This book is dedicated to anyone who is healing.

DANCE
with me

A *With Me In Seattle* Novel

KRISTEN PROBY

Cover Art by:
Hang Le

Cover Photography by:
Sara Eirew Photographer

Interior Design & Formatting by:
Christine Borgford

The Romancing Manhattan Series:

All the Way

All It Takes

ALSO AVAILABLE
Kristen Proby's Crossover Collection:

Wicked Force:
A Wicked Horse Vegas / Big Sky Novella
by Sawyer Bennett

All Stars Fall:
A Seaside Pictures / Big Sky Novella
by Rachel Van Dyken

Hold On:
A Play On / Big Sky Novella
by Samantha Young

Worth Fighting For:
A Warrior Fight Club / Big Sky Novella
by Laura Kaye

Crazy Imperfect Love:
A Dirty Dicks / Big Sky Novella
by K.L. Grayson

Nothing Without You:
A Forever Yours / Big Sky Novella
by Monica Murphy

prologue

Starla

"You like that?" he growls into my ear, his eyes pinned to mine in the mirror in front of us.

We're on the bed, Levi's back is against the headboard, and I'm braced against his hard, muscled chest. He's spread my legs wide open, and I'm watching with rapt fascination as his hands glide over my skin, making me long in ways I haven't in what feels like mellennia.

"Oh, yeah," I breathe, biting my lip when he nibbles my earlobe. "I like it."

"What about this?"

His fingers pluck my pussy lips like guitar strings, and my hips circle in an invitation for more.

Dear God, give me more!

"Mm, seems that hit a nerve."

"About forty million nerves." I'm breathless. My naked breasts heave as I pant, my nipples puckered from the pinching he doled out just minutes ago.

Jesus, who knew a little pain was so fucking delicious?

"Look at that," he murmurs, and we both watch as those talented fingers dip inside me, then come out glistening in the low glow of the sidelight. "You're wet, sweetheart."

"Shocker." He grins at me in the mirror and pushes two fingers back inside me. My first reaction is to close my legs, to press against his flesh, chasing the orgasm he's held just out of my reach.

"Not yet." He urges my legs out again and drags his wet fingers over my hard, pulsing clit. "Soon."

Who knew the sexy cop I just met today could make me feel so uninhibited? So reckless?

So damn *wanton*?

He doesn't ask permission, he just takes and takes without apology, and it's so damn *sexy*. Everyone's always so careful with me. So timid.

Don't upset the pop star.

But he's taking the decisions out of my hands, and rather than feeling threatened in any way, I feel *free*.

Sexy.

Wanted.

"Stop thinking so hard," he growls. "Just watch."

"If you don't fuck me,"—I swallow hard—"I'm going to die."

He smiles, a full-on, wide grin as if what I just said pleases him to his core, and the next thing I know, he's moved out from behind me. He grabs my ankle and yanks me down onto my back, then covers me in one swift motion.

"You move fast for such a big man."

"Reflexes are part of my job." He's braced over me on hard, muscled arms. "What do you want, Starla?"

"You." It's really that simple—and that scary. For the first time in roughly five years, I want a man more than I want my next breath.

"How?"

I circle my hips, grinding against his hard, long cock and grin when he clenches his jaw and swears under his breath.

"You're a big boy. Figure it out."

His dark eyes are hot with lust and need as he reaches over for a condom, and flips me onto my belly.

I hear the tear of the packet, and I start to raise my ass into the air, but he plants his hand on my lower back and presses me to the mattress.

"Stay."

"You're damn bossy."

He straddles my thighs and presses his front to my back. Without lowering his weight onto me, he talks directly into my ear.

"If you want me to stop, speak up now."

"Don't stop."

It's not a plea, it's a direct order, and by the feel of Levi's grin against my ear, he approves.

He sits up and spreads my ass cheeks apart with his thumbs, but rather than sink inside me, he slides his hard cock back and forth along my wet slit, spreading the juices around until I'm back to DEFCON 5 in the arousal department.

"Levi."

"That's right." He slides inside me, seating himself comfortably despite his size, thanks to how damn turned on I am. "You're with me."

Trust me, I haven't forgotten.

And when he starts to truly fuck me, not holding back in the least, pushing and stretching until all I can do is fist my hands in the pillow and scream my release with abandon, I know I'll never have another experience like this one.

He braces an arm on the headboard above me as he continues to move, until finally, with a low groan, he finds his own release.

This is most likely where the uncomfortable awkwardness will set in. Let's face it, I met Levi today through a friend—okay, my *best* friend, but still—and brought him back to my hotel suite after my sold-out concert. We didn't waste any time with small talk.

No, he jumped right to the good stuff, God bless him.

So, I won't be surprised if he grabs his clothes, thanks me, and heads out.

But once he's cleaned himself up, he returns to the bed, covers us both up, and pulls me to him.

He's warm and firm, and I admit he feels damn good. No one's held me like this in a *long* time. That thought doesn't hurt the way it used to. It's just a small ache now, and that makes me feel guilty.

I always feel guilty.

"You don't have to stay," I blurt, then frown.

"You want me to leave?"

"No." I let out a gusty sigh. "Honestly, I just don't want you to think you have to stay. I'm giving you an out."

"Thanks." He kisses my forehead and hugs me close. "Out received and declined."

His comment makes me feel better. Less cheap.

Levi's body is loose and calm. His fingers slowly comb through my hair, making me a little sleepy, which is unexpected because I rarely sleep.

"You're thinking again."

He doesn't look down at me, and it gives me an opportunity to check out his sharp jawline, covered in just a little scruff.

He probably shaved earlier in the day. It's well after midnight now.

"How did you get this scar?" I trace the white line on his chin.

"Knife," he says, not elaborating.

I sketch his jawline with my fingertip, up around the lobe of his ear, then over the few gray strands of hair at his temple.

"You have some gray."

"That's the job," he says simply. "And age."

"You're not that old."

"Over forty," he says with a grin. "But not ancient."

"I'm on the shady side of thirty-five myself," I admit with a small smile. "Of course, we tell the media differently."

"Of course," he repeats.

"I like the gray. It's sexy."

He captures my hand and kisses it, then rolls me onto my back and buries his face against my neck, biting and kissing the delicate flesh there.

"Touch me like that, and it turns into this."

"I wasn't touching you in a sexy way."

"You were touching me," he says simply. "That's all it seems to take with you."

$\backsim$

"THE HOTEL IN Phoenix is ready, and security has already

cleared it," my assistant, Rachel, says. We're sitting on my plane, and she's filling me in on the details of our next city for the tour.

This is typical for us. We catch up on our way to the next place. I usually forget where I am once I'm there.

Except for Seattle because I have my closest friends there. Meredith and Jax used to tour with me back in the day, but now they have families of their own, and I'm still doing this: singing, writing, touring.

I'm never home. I don't know why I bought the huge house in Hollywood.

"The crew is setting up at the venue now, and when we land, we'll go straight there for sound check."

"I need a couple of hours this afternoon to rest," I inform her.

Her brunette head rises in surprise. I never request time for myself.

"We can work that in. You do always get what you want, after all."

"What does that mean?" Of course I get what I want. I pay your salary.

"I'm just kidding. You're the boss."

"Is that everything?" I smile, but her comment stings. I'm not a diva. Not nearly as bad as other famous people I've seen.

"I think so." She closes her laptop and stares at me.

"Just ask whatever it is that's on your mind."

"I don't know what you mean."

I roll my eyes. Rachel's been with me for three years. She knows me incredibly well, and aside from Meredith and Jax, she might be one of the few people I trust with the details of my life.

"Okay, did you sleep with that hot guy last night?"

"Yeah."

"Whoa."

"What?"

"You never do that. Like, ever."

"I know." I swallow and cross one leg over the other. I'm so damn sore today, it's ridiculous.

"Are you going to see him again?"

I shrug, unsure of how to respond. Just then, my phone pings with an incoming text.

"Speak of the devil," I mutter but don't read the message with Rachel sitting next to me. She waits for a heartbeat.

"Aren't you going to read it?"

"Not with your nosy ass sitting here."

She pouts but moves to a seat on the other side of the plane. "You're no fun."

I shake my head and open the text.

You didn't answer me this morning. Talk to me.

I bite my lip and close the message without replying. I stare out the window, at the clouds and the mountains below.

I like Levi. I *want* him. And that hasn't happened in a long time.

But I'm also broken, and he deserves better. So it's for the best that we just go our separate ways, calling last night exactly what it was.

A one-night stand.

one

Starla

"I don't sleep."

The doctor frowns as he types something into his cheap laptop.

"Why is that?"

Oh, I don't know . . . nightmares from watching the love of my life die in front of my eyes? Guilt? Anger? Unbearable sadness? Pick one.

But I don't say any of that out loud.

"Insomnia," I reply and have to close my eyes against the wave of dizziness that settles over me every three minutes or so.

"How long has the dizziness been happening?"

I fucking hate going to the doctor. I literally just told his nurse all of this ten minutes ago. Now I have to say it all over again, and it makes me stabby. Most singing artists have a doctor on staff, but I don't. I'm just . . . fine. And maybe a little pissy.

Of course, I've been moody for about five years now.

Finally, a couple of days ago, I called my producer and asked him to recommend someone. A physician excellent at caring for vocal health, who also understands the art of discretion.

"A couple of months," I reply and cough into my hand. My voice is still raspy from the tour I just wrapped up. "It didn't happen often at first, but it's getting worse. And the last week or so, it's happened on stage, and I can't have that. Everything is choreographed down to the tiniest detail, and I can't be off. I don't want to get hurt."

"I agree with you there," he says and finally looks me in the eyes and smiles. "Let's figure this out, shall we?"

"Yes, please."

He pokes and prods, checking out my glands, looking up my nose, listening to me breathe. The usual routine at the doctor's, whether you're there for a headache or the plague.

I cough again when he asks me to breathe deep.

"How long have you had the cough?"

"It's a side effect of my job," I say, clearing my throat. "I just came off of a thirteen-month tour, singing pretty much every night of the week."

"And that's finished now?"

"For about two weeks," I confirm with a nod. "And then I go back into the studio."

"When was the last time you took a break?"

I shake my head. "I don't take breaks."

He sets his computer aside, pushes his glasses up his nose, and looks me dead in the eyes.

"Starla, everyone needs to take a break. Especially someone like you, whose job is so physically demanding."

"I have a career to manage," I reply simply. "I have a staff to pay."

"What about your family?"

I raise a brow. "That's none of your business."

He lets out a sigh. "I'm not trying to be nosy here. What I'm saying is, you *need* to rest. Your vocal cords, your body. Even emotionally, you need it. I'd also like to address your weight."

"I'm not overweight," I say immediately. "I'm muscular."

"You're *under*weight," he says. "Do you have a chef?"

"I have catering for everyone," I reply, evading the question.

"That's not what I asked you."

"I eat when I'm hungry. I don't drink coffee or alcohol. I'm not unhealthy."

"You need to sleep and eat, and you need a break," he says firmly. "I've worked in this industry for years, Starla. You're not the first famous singer to walk into my office. I've been doing this for twenty years, and I'm telling you, this is classic exhaustion."

"I don't have a brain tumor?" I ask softly, finally expressing my worst nightmare.

"I highly doubt it," he says. "You need to take three months off."

"*Three months*?" I stand and pace the small exam room. "I can't take that kind of time. Every day is scheduled. That would mean cancelling appearances."

"No concerts," he says again. "If you're slated at awards shows, that's fine, but no full concerts. No studio time. You're a superstar, Starla. A few months off isn't going to kill your career."

No, but it might kill me.

"I don't believe this," I mutter and sit in a chair when the dizziness comes. "I hate being dizzy."

"It's not fun," he agrees. "And your voice sounds overextended. All of these years of hard work have taken their toll."

"I'm only thirty-six," I remind him. "I'm hardly ready to retire."

"I'm not suggesting retirement," he says with a kind smile. "But I'm writing a prescription for ninety days away from work. Go on vacation. Visit someone. Do anything, except sing.

"Come back after those ninety days, and we'll reassess. If the dizziness doesn't get better in the next week or so, call me. But I think after a few days, it'll be much better."

"Can it be that simple?"

"Rest isn't simple. As you know, or you'd do it more often."

I nod, and after he prescribes me sleeping aids that I won't take, I put my hat and sunglasses on and hurry out to my car.

I didn't see any paparazzi when I arrived, but we're in Hollywood. You never know when and where they'll pop up, and I don't need TMZ splashing *Starla leaves renowned doctor's office—is her career over?* all over the place.

Once I'm in the car and headed toward my house in the hills, I call Meredith.

"How did it go?" she asks. It sounds like she's chewing on something. "Sorry, hold on. Do *not* hit her with that!"

I laugh, imagining what's going on in Meredith's house in Seattle.

"Sorry about that. How was it?"

"Horrible."

"Oh, God. Star, do you have a tumor?"

"I don't think so. He says I need to *rest*." I roll my eyes and turn up the road to my house. "As in, no performing or record-ing for *three months*."

"Awesome," she says, making me scowl.

"Not awesome."

"No, it kind of is. You need a break."

I drive through the gate to my house and park in the garage.

"Why does everyone think they know what's best for me? I don't need to rest, I need to work."

I grab my Hermes bag and climb out of the Mercedes, then have to brace myself against the side of the car when the dizziness returns.

"Oh, fuck."

"Breathe," she says soothingly. "Seriously, this is perfect timing. You just wrapped up the tour. No one expects you to jump back into another one after that. It's been too many months of non-stop concerts."

If I don't work, I dwell. I don't want to do that.

"What the hell am I supposed to do for three months?"

"Sleep. Write music. Shop. Go to the movies. Eat pizza. Should I continue?"

"Okay, so those things don't sound so bad. Particularly the shopping."

I set my bag on the kitchen counter and sit on a stool at the massive island. This house is ridiculously enormous, especially for just one person. I've never cooked in this kitchen.

I'm never here.

"I'm going to be so fucking bored."

"I have the best idea ever," she says. I can hear the excitement in her voice. "Come to Seattle. You can dance with Jax and me to stay in shape, and you'll have us nearby. You don't have anyone in LA. Not really."

She's not wrong, and I don't know if I should be sad about that. I have acquaintances here, and a few friends, but no one that I trust the way I do Meredith and Jax.

"I love you, but I don't want to live with you," I reply with a laugh. "No offense."

"None taken," she says. "Jax and Logan just bought a house that looks over the Sound, near Natalie's old place. I know Nat's place is empty, and she'll totally let you live there for a while."

"Are you sure? That seems like a huge imposition."

"No, it's really not. That house sits empty most of the time unless someone in the family needs it. Whenever they think about selling, someone wants to use it. It's like the Universe is against Nat selling it or something."

"If she's okay with it, that might be perfect. And it's near Jax and Logan?"

"Yep, right up the street. And I'm only twenty minutes away. It's perfect."

"I don't think I should drive up." I nibble my lip. "Not while I'm dizzy like this."

"I'm sure someone here has a car you can borrow."

"Dude, I have more money than Midas. I could just buy one when I get there."

"Fun! Car shopping." I can hear the excitement in her voice, and it makes me excited, too. The thought of being close to her for several months isn't a horrible thing.

"Go ahead and call Natalie, see if it's available." I bite my lip, thinking it over while I look around the big, white kitchen. "Why did I buy this huge house again?"

"Investment. And you have to have a home base," she says. "Also, that closet. I could live in your damn closet."

"Ah, yes," I say with a smile. "The closet. Anyway, I have to call Donald and fill him in so he can get the word out that I won't need the studio. And I hate to say it, but we have some shows to cancel."

Donald is my manager, and will *not* be happy about this change in plans.

"I know you hate it. But, Star, it's for the best."

"If you say so."

"GOOD GOD, YOU'VE been here for a week, and you're already getting more deliveries than me," Jax says as he walks inside the house in Seattle that Natalie is leasing to me while I'm on medical leave. Donald worked out all of the details for my recording and performance schedule, and I'm officially on an extended vacation.

The best part is, Jax and his husband Logan are right down the street. They come over often for dinner or breakfast or just to chat.

Jax carries two boxes stacked on top of each other, and Logan has two plastic bags full of Chipotle.

"I'm actually hungry," I say as they join me in the dining room that looks out over the pool in the backyard. The house is gorgeous, and the view of the Sound from the upstairs is even better. I'll be writing plenty of songs up there.

"So your office is sending up your fan mail?" Logan asks as he opens a box. Inside is a pile of letters and gifts.

"Yeah, they're sending it once a week." I pull a burrito out of the bag and take a big bite. I've eaten more since I've been here than I did a whole month on the road. I'm *always* hungry now, which is new for me.

It also means that I feel a few extra pounds making their

way onto my frame. I need to get back to working out.

But whether I like to admit it or not, the dizziness is less frequent. So, maybe some time off and away from the chaos that is a pop star's life is exactly what I needed.

"Okay, let's read them," Jax says as he reaches for an envelope. "Dear Starla, I'm your biggest fan ever. *Dance With Me* is my favorite song, and I sing it all the time to my kids."

Jax looks up at me and bats his eyelashes. "Aww, so sweet."

"Don't be a dick." I toss a chip at him, but he catches it out of the air and pops it into his mouth.

"Listen to this one," Logan says, joining in on the fun. "Dear Starla, I don't usually write letters like this—"

"Which is code for they write them all the time," Jax adds.

"—but I need to tell you that your music has changed my life. I started dancing, at home at first, but then at the gym in an Oula class when I got more confident. I've lost a hundred and twenty pounds."

"Holy shit," Jax says and whistles through his teeth. "I take it back, that's a cool letter."

"Very cool," I agree before taking another big bite of my burrito. "What's in that puffy envelope?"

Jax reaches for it and opens it, revealing a necklace in a black velvet pouch. The pendant is half of a heart that says *Best*.

"I'm assuming whoever sent this kept the *friend* part?" Jax asks.

"Is that creepy to anyone but me?" I ask thoughtfully.

"Kinda creepy," Logan agrees. "But maybe it's a young girl."

"If that's the case, it's not creepy." I nod in agreement.

"How are things?" Jax asks, finally setting aside the letters and opening his own burrito. "How are you feeling?"

"A little better," I admit. "The house is great. Seeing you guys helps, too."

"She loves us," Jax says to Logan, who just smirks. They've been married for more than five years now. I can't believe how fast the time has gone. Back in the early days of my career, Jax and Meredith were dancers on my first tour. They've choreographed every show since, even though they don't travel anymore. They've settled down in Seattle, running a dance studio and loving their lives.

They're my best friends in the world, and I miss them. Meredith was totally right to suggest I spend a few months here. I would be going nuts in that mausoleum I own in LA.

"Are you resting like the doctor told you to?" Logan asks. He's the more laid back of the two of them. But both are stupidly attractive.

"I've never slept well," I reply honestly. "But I'm not dancing and singing my ass off every night anymore. I'm taking it easy."

"Dizzy?" Jax asks.

"Nope. It's gotten better. So I'm ready to get back into the studio and dance."

Logan frowns. "Is that a good idea?"

"I'll take it easy on her," Jax says, watching me. He knows me. "She should stay active so she doesn't lose her fitness level."

"Exactly," I agree. "And so I don't resort to murder."

"That would be unfortunate." Logan chuckles and wads his empty wrapper in his hands, then tosses it into the bag it came in. "Let me read another letter from an admirer."

"I want admirers," Jax says.

"I admire you, darling," Logan replies, blowing his husband a kiss.

"You guys are ridiculously adorable." I laugh as I shut the lid on the letters. "I'll go through these later."

"They should sort them for you," Jax says. "Like, read ahead and categorize them in case there's anything creepy in there."

"Like an earlobe or something?" I ask with a raised brow.

"Ew. No, serial killer. Like just weird stalker-type stuff."

Like the email I got this morning.

I clear my throat, and Jax's eyes narrow.

"What happened?"

"What are you talking about? Nothing."

He shakes his head, and Logan's gaze bounces back and forth between us.

"What's up?" Logan asks.

"Nothing," I repeat.

"You're a bad liar," Jax says.

"Stop harassing me. You'll make me dizzy."

"You're going to milk that for all it's worth, aren't you?"

I smile angelically and pop another chip into my mouth.

"When do we get to dance?" I ask, changing the subject.

"Today, if you want."

"I want."

"That's my cue to get back to work," Logan says, standing and gathering our mess to throw away. "I'll see you later. Are we still going car shopping tomorrow?"

"If you have time, yes," I say with a smile. "I need some wheels, and I'm feeling well enough to drive. Finally."

"Then wheels the lady shall have," Logan replies. He kisses Jax, then gives me a hug and walks out.

"He's hot." My voice is casual in a matter-of-fact way.

"Girl, you have no idea," Jax replies with a laugh. He cues

up some music on his phone and scoots the couch out of the way, giving us plenty of space on the hardwood floor to dance.

"I love that we can do this anywhere."

"Me, too."

The music starts, pulsing through the room. The song isn't one of mine, which I prefer. I don't want this to feel like work.

We immediately move into an old routine from my previous tour. It's not acrobatic, which is good as my muscles loosen, warming up.

Jax takes my hand and spins me to him, then lifts me and sets me down again. God, the music feels *amazing*.

I've missed this. Dancing for the fun of it. For the love of it.

The song finishes, but we continue through two more.

When the final song ends, I'm panting, my hands planted on my hips.

"I've only been out of the game for two weeks."

"That'll do it," he says, passing me a towel to wipe the sweat off my face. "You'll get it back quickly."

"I hope so." I sigh and immediately start to stretch. I don't want to cramp up. "But it's okay if I'm not tour-ready for a while."

"I agree. I'm glad you're taking some time off."

I nod, but I don't know that I'd call what I feel *glad*. There's relief there, for sure. Always mixed with some guilt.

Jax gathers his things and kisses my forehead. "I have to get to class. Do you need anything, little girl?"

I grin. He's called me *little girl* for years. "No, I'm good."

"I'll call you later."

He waves, and then he's gone. I start to march up the stairs to take a shower, but the doorbell rings.

"Did you forget something?" I call out with a smile and jog over to the door, opening it without looking through the peephole.

Only it's not Jax on the other side.

It's Levi.

Levi from that night several months ago. The best sex of my life, Levi.

What the hell is he doing here?

"Hello, Starla."

"Well, shit."

two

Levi

❝ **T**his is heavy as fuck," I grunt as I help my brother Wyatt push a wrought iron bench across the concrete of his pool area. "Why did you pick out the heaviest stuff they had?"

"I didn't pick it out," he says. "My gorgeous wife did."

"Figures." Wyatt motions for me to stop. I stand and prop my hands on my hips, surveying the area. Despite the size and sheer weight of the new pool furniture, I have to concede that it looks nice. "Where are the cushions?"

"Back here."

I follow him around the side of the house where the cushions are stacked and waiting to be placed. By the time we haul them and get them set up, we're both panting.

"Even the cushions are heavy," Wyatt says with a laugh. "The store offered to deliver and set up, but it's just patio furniture. How hard can it be?"

"Hard enough to pay the store to do the work." I shake my head and wipe my brow with the handkerchief I keep in my back pocket. "You owe me a beer."

"I can pay that debt."

I follow him into the house and sit at the kitchen island. Wyatt grabs two bottles of beer from his beverage fridge, pops the tops, and passes me one.

"Thanks for your help."

"You're welcome." I take a pull on the beer. It's cold and refreshing on my dry throat, so I take another drink. "Where is Lia?"

"She's in L.A. for a couple of days, going over marketing plans for her new makeup line."

"Good for her." I'm proud of my new sister-in-law. What started as a hobby—showing women how to apply their makeup on YouTube—has grown into millions of fans and a seven-figure makeup deal. Lia's living her dream.

"It launches just before Christmas."

"Excellent timing. Not that I know how the retail world works, but Christmas has to be a good time."

"Agreed." Wyatt smiles and drinks his beer. "How have you been?"

Exhausted.

"Busy," I say instead. "It seems the good people of Seattle enjoy ripping each other off."

I am a detective in the property crimes division of the Seattle Police Department.

The shit I see on a daily basis would make anyone lose their faith in humanity.

"Job security, right?"

"I suppose."

"You don't love this new job."

I sigh and shrug a shoulder. I transferred to this division about two years ago. "There's an opening in homicide. I'm thinking of throwing my hat in for it."

"Homicide." My brother raises a brow. "You'll be all gray by the end of the year."

"Funny." I stand and pace his kitchen, thinking it over. "I think I need a new challenge. I've been interested in homicide for a long time."

"Well, I hope you get it, then." His eyes tell me there's something more.

"But?"

"You already live and breathe the job," he reminds me. "Homicide would be more."

"Depends on how many people turn up dead."

"You know what I mean."

I stand with my back to him, looking out his front windows toward the house across the street. The house Lia lived in when Wyatt met her.

There's a car parked out front, making me frown. "I thought that house was empty?"

"It usually is," he confirms. "But Natalie Williams is letting Starla stay there for a few months."

My gaze whips to my brother's, and he cringes.

"I was looking for the right time to tell you."

"Jesus." I set my half-empty bottle on a nearby table and shove my hands into my pockets. "It's not that big of a deal."

It's a big fucking deal.

"Bullshit," he says. Wyatt's really the only one who knows that after I spent the night with Starla, I tried to contact her, but she ghosted me.

It was humiliating. I didn't consider what we did to be a one-night stand.

One-night stands don't feel like that.

But she never replied to my texts, and I wasn't willing to beg for her attention.

"How long has she been there?"

"A week."

I turn to him now and raise a brow.

"I know, I should have called you. But she messed you up, man. I—"

"You should have called me. If the roles were reversed, you'd be pissed."

He blows out a breath and hangs his head. "Yeah. You're right."

I look back at the house, just as a man leaves and walks down to his car, whistling.

"Who the fuck is that?"

"Jax," Wyatt says immediately. "You've met him, remember? He's married to Logan?"

I consciously make my hands relax and nod stiffly. "Right."

"Dude, you've got it bad. Jax is her friend. If you want to stake a claim, go do it."

Been there, done that. Have the broken heart to show for it.

I shrug. "That ship has sailed. Enjoy your new pool furniture. Tell Lia I said hi."

"Will do. Keep me posted about the homicide thing."

"I will."

I wave and walk out toward my 4-Runner, but stop and shake my head in frustration.

She's twenty yards from me, for Christ's sake.

Without overthinking it, I march across the street and ring the doorbell.

I hear her say something from inside, but I can't make out the words. And then she flings open the door, and her happy smile changes into wide-eyed shock.

"Hello, Starla."

"Well, shit."

M y eyes soak her in from head to toe. How did she get more beautiful than before? Her auburn hair is pulled up in a knot on top of her head, and she's in a cropped T-shirt with a pair of skin-tight shorts.

My dick is immediately at full attention.

"Wh-what are you doing here?"

"I was over at Wyatt's house." I point across the street. "And he said you were staying here."

She leans on the doorframe, crosses her arms over her chest, and bites her full bottom lip.

She's sex personified, standing right in front of me.

"Am I under arrest?"

"No." I reach out to brush a loose strand of hair behind her ear, and the slight contact of skin against skin sends a shock wave through my already energized body. "No, you basically fell in my lap, and I decided to take advantage of it."

"If you think I'm going to lead you straight up to bed, you have another thing coming."

I narrow my eyes. "You just insulted both of us."

She sighs and shakes her head, pinches the bridge of her nose between her eyes, and then laughs. "I apologize. You surprised me. Come on in."

She stands back, and I follow her in, looking around the

open living space.

"Do you want something to drink?"

"No, thanks."

"I need a water. Follow me."

She walks ahead of me to the kitchen, and my eyes are pinned to her round ass. I remember how the globes of those cheeks feel in my hands as she rides me. I remember *everything*.

"Sure you don't want some?"

I try to swallow around my dry tongue and just nod. "Turns out, I do."

She passes me a bottle and then takes a sip of her own.

"So, is the tour over?" I ask.

"Yes, and I'm on vacation." She frowns slightly, staring down at her water. "Forced vacation."

"Why?"

She blinks up at me. "Because I was exhausted, and the doctor insisted."

I narrow my eyes again, pissed that she worked herself into exhaustion. "Starla—"

"I'm fine," she insists. "And I'm already feeling better. Also, I owe you an apology."

That stops me short. "No, you don't."

"Oh, I do." She takes another sip, then sets the bottle aside and leans on the island. I get a great view of her cleavage.

She's too sexy for her own damn good.

"I'm sorry I didn't reply to your messages, Levi."

"Why didn't you?"

She blows out a breath. "Because I was a little overwhelmed. The sex was—"

"Damn incredible."

"Yeah. It was. Intense is also a good word for it, and I get the feeling that you're an intense man."

I nod once. "If I hurt you or scared you—"

"No, it's not that at all," she hurries to assure me. "I didn't do anything that I didn't want or enjoy. I'm sorry if I gave you that impression. I hadn't been with a man in a long time, and we have some powerful chemistry."

That's the understatement of the year. I can feel the electricity flowing between us like a rushing river.

"That's really all I'm comfortable saying right now," she admits and swallows.

"That's enough."

For now.

"Are you safe?"

Her eyes are wide again as she stares at me, flustered by the question.

"Yeah. I am."

"Good." I nod and then turn to leave, but before I get to the door, I decide *fuck it* and turn back to her. "I'll pick you up at seven for dinner. Casual."

"Levi."

I raise a brow, and she smiles.

"I'll be ready."

"MER'S TALKED ABOUT this place," Starla says after I park and open the door for her. "She says they have the best burgers in Seattle."

"Red Mill is the best," I agree with a smile and link my

fingers with hers as we cross the parking lot to the front of the building. It's tiny, usually with a line out the door. The restaurant only boasts about ten tables, so seating is a challenge.

Miraculously, we've come at a good time because we get right in to order, and find a corner table to eat.

"This is . . . *cute.*" She wrinkles her nose as she looks around.

"I know it seems like a greasy spoon place, but just wait until you taste this burger. You'll be in heaven."

"Do you come here often?" She braces her chin on her hand and watches me with happy blue eyes. Her lashes are long, but she's not wearing any makeup. Her auburn hair is tucked up in a blond wig, which made me laugh when she opened the door earlier.

"Only a few times a year. Any more than that, it would become an addiction."

"You guys have built it up so big, what if I don't love it?"

"You will."

My name is called, so I fetch our dinner, set the tray on the table, and we retrieve our orders.

Starla immediately bites into her burger, and I watch, waiting to see her reaction.

She chews, then sighs in delight.

"Smm gmmd."

I take a bite and laugh. "What was that?"

"So good." She wipes her mouth and pops a fry. "If the house next door was for sale, I'd buy it so I could eat here every day."

"See? Addictive. I wouldn't steer you wrong."

"I believe you."

We're quiet as we eat. I was hungrier than I thought, and concentrating on eating takes the focus away from wanting to strip her bare and have my way with her.

I don't remember ever feeling this *carnal* about a woman. I've wanted my fair share, but it's never been a primal need.

Until her.

And it seems the weeks since I last saw her didn't diminish the need in the least. If anything, it intensified it. But I'm not going to scare her away this time. So, even if it kills me—and it just might—I'm going to take my time with her.

"My fries are gone." She pouts, then eyes my basket. I slide it toward her.

"Help yourself."

"I don't want to eat your dinner."

"Okay."

I move to pull it back, but she snatches it away, making me laugh.

"But if you're going to offer, I don't want to hurt your feelings." She winks at me and takes a few of my fries. "You and Mer were right. This place is the bomb."

"We'll come back."

Her back is to the room, and my eyes constantly move around the space, keeping a tally of who's here and where they are.

"Do you ever turn the cop off?" she wonders as she finishes my fries.

"No."

She cocks a brow. "Ever? Because you weren't very cop-like that night."

"I'm always a cop," I say simply. "Whether I'm in my office or inside you, that doesn't change."

Her cheeks pinken as she takes a sip of her drink. "It's

fascinating to watch you in public."

"Why?"

"You're always watchful."

"Part of that is habit, and part of it is because I'm with you."

She tips her head to the side. "Why me?"

"Because you're you, and your safety is always my top priority."

"Listen, if what I do for a living makes you uncomfortable—"

"It doesn't," I assure her. "But you can't deny that going out in public makes you a target. You're wearing a disguise for God's sake."

"I wear it all the time. It's just easier."

"And it's habit for me to know the room." I take her hand. "Regardless if you're famous or the girl next door, your safety is the priority."

"So, chivalry isn't dead after all."

She smiles, lighting up the whole fucking room.

"It shouldn't be. My mama raised me right."

"Remind me to thank her."

She frowns as if she shouldn't have said that, but I bring her fingers to my lips and kiss her knuckles. "I'll do that. Shall we go?"

"Sure, they probably need the table."

We gather our trash and dump it on the way out of the building. One younger girl does a double-take at Starla, but I hurry her out of the restaurant and to my vehicle.

I drive back across the city to Alki Beach where Starla's staying. The sun is about to set.

"It's a pretty day," she says with a sigh, watching the city pass by.

"Summer's almost over," I reply.

"Time flies," she murmurs, and then we're quiet the rest of the way to her place. I park in the driveway, but rather than lead her to her door, I stop on the sidewalk.

"Take a walk with me?"

She nods happily. "It's too nice to go inside."

I link her fingers with mine, and we walk the block or so down to the waterfront, wandering along the paved path. Families are having picnic dinners, couples walk and wait for the sunset.

Kites fly, boats float past.

It's something out of a postcard.

"It smells good," Starla says, taking a deep breath.

When we've reached the end of the public beach, I lead her to an empty bench. We sit, and she immediately scoots next to me, leaning into me and resting her head on my shoulder. Jesus, she fits perfectly right here next to me, like a puzzle piece.

"I'm going to take this walk every evening," she says as if she's talking to herself. I want to warn her not to, that she's too recognizable to walk here alone. But she's a grown woman, and if a walk along the waterfront makes her happy, who am I to tell her no?

I'll just make sure I'm here to walk with her.

"The sun is slipping away," she murmurs.

The sky is a riot of purple and orange, painting a gorgeous picture for us. I'm as comfortable and content as I've ever been. The exhaustion and frustration from the past few months has lifted after just a couple of hours of being with this woman.

After the sun slides into the water, we stand and start the walk back to her place. The sky is a deep purple when we reach her door.

"Do you want to come in?" she asks.

I lean on the doorframe and sigh. "I want to come in more than I want to breathe, but I won't. Not tonight."

I drag my fingertips down her smooth cheek.

"Okay." Her eyes fall to my lips. I won't sleep with her tonight, but I'm no saint. I can't keep my lips away from her. From the look in her baby blue eyes, I'd say she wants a kiss as much as I do.

I frame her neck and jaw in my hands and lean into her. Her lips touch mine, and I'm gone, slipping into the sweet haze of lust that comes whenever I'm close to her.

She holds onto my sides as if she needs something to ground her as I plunder her mouth, exploring, reacquainting myself with her.

She's sweet. Sexy.

Delicious.

But I slowly pull away and smile down at her.

"Thank you for going to dinner with me tonight."

She licks her lips, surely still tasting me there.

"Thanks for asking me."

I laugh. "I think I told you."

"I could have said no."

I cock a brow. "Could you?"

"I could." She clears her throat and squares her shoulders. Her sassiness turns me on even more. "I'm attracted to you, Levi. I *like* you. But make no mistake, I'm a strong woman, and if I didn't want you here, I would tell you so."

I nod and kiss her forehead. "Good."

She opens the door to walk into the house and glances back

at me with a smile.

"I'll text you tomorrow. I'd appreciate a reply."

"I can do that."

She closes the door, and I walk to my 4-Runner. I'm not ready to go home, but Wyatt's busy with a deadline, so walking over to his place is out of the question.

I shoot our other brother, Jace, a text.

Are you home?

I pull out of Starla's driveway and head back toward my place, a condo in the heart of downtown. It's convenient to work.

I'm at a stop sign when Jace replies.

Sorry, no. At the hospital. Emergency?

I shoot off a quick reply. *No. I'll be over for breakfast.*

Jace sends back the thumbs-up emoji. It seems I'm headed home, after all.

three

Starla

I freaking *love* this car," Meredith says while bouncing in the passenger seat of my new ride. "Jaguars don't suck."

"No. They don't." I laugh at my friend and fiddle with the air conditioning. "Summer sure is hanging in there."

"This is definitely warm for September," she agrees. "But I'm not complaining because soon, it'll be cold and rainy. I'm enjoying every minute of summer."

"Good point." I merge onto the freeway, driving away from Meredith's home in the suburbs toward downtown. She picked me up this morning, and we bought this new little F-Type. I like the sporty feel of the car, and that it has so much get up and go.

Once the purchase was finished, I followed Mer back to her place where we dropped off her car and hopped in my new one, ready to go shopping in downtown Seattle.

"Thanks for going with me," I say with a smile. "Jax and Logan had something come up today."

"Oh, it was entirely my pleasure to watch you work that

salesman. He didn't know what hit him."

"I'm just good at getting my way when I need to." I hook my hair behind my ear. "And if he thought I was going to pay that much over MSRP just because I *can*, he clearly doesn't know me."

"Well, he does now," she replies. "And you have a killer car."

"Where should we go first?" I check the time on the dash. "We lost the morning to car shopping."

"Let's go to the market last," she says, referring to Pike's Place Market. "I'll want fresh flowers, and they won't survive in the car."

"Good call. Me, too. Retail therapy then?"

"Hell, yes." She shimmies in the seat. "I told Mark I was about to do some serious damage to the credit card."

"Does he care about stuff like that?"

"Not really, I just like to torment him." She points to the parking garage under Nordstrom. "I'd park in there. It's central and safe."

"Perfect."

Once we're parked and inside the building, it's like Christmas. We walk through all of the luxury shops: Louis Vuitton, Chanel, and Gucci among others. I find a *gorgeous* bag in Chanel but leave without it, deciding to think about it.

"I don't know why you passed that up," Meredith says as she sips on her Starbucks, holding her own Louis Vuitton shopping bag. "It's seriously so you."

"I know, but I also liked the bag in Gucci."

She raises a brow. "Star, I don't know if you know this, but you can afford it."

I cringe. "I know, but it seems self-indulgent."

"You just came off a thirteen-month tour where you worked yourself into *exhaustion*." She shakes her head. "Seriously, if you want to buy the damn bags, buy them. All of them. Enjoy them."

I'm watching her, soaking in what she's saying. "Why am I so bad at rewarding myself for a job well done?"

"Oh, you don't have time for that level of therapy." She sips her drink. "I could sit here and list twenty reasons just off the top of my head."

"I never used to have a hard time spoiling myself."

"That was before," she says quietly, watching me with those big blue eyes. "Since then, you've done nothing but punish yourself."

I think about Levi, that night after the show and yesterday, and feel a smile slowly spread over my face.

"You're holding out on me," she says, grabbing my arm. "Spill it. Right now. Or I won't be your friend anymore."

"Liar." I laugh and sip my frap as we walk back toward Nordy's and the shops where I've decided to spend a *ridiculous* amount of money. "You'd never desert me. You love me too much."

"Okay, that's true," she concedes. "But you have to tell me."

"Well, you're right in that I've carried guilt. I'm still carrying it, but I think it's fading a bit over time."

"Get to the good stuff."

"You're so impatient." I laugh as I hold the door open for her, and we walk into the blessedly air-conditioned building. "And this is not a conversation to be had while I buy out Chanel."

"Later then. In the car. I need to know everything."

"Deal."

I walk to the sales associate who was helping us earlier and smile.

"You're back," she says warmly. I like her. She never made a fuss about who I am, even though I could see in her eyes from the minute we walked in that she recognized me.

"We are," I agree and point to the bag that caught my eye. "And I've come back for her."

"It's such a great piece to add to your collection," she says with a smile and reaches in a cupboard for one that hasn't been on display.

"But that's not all." I smile at Mer, who nods in support. "There's another one over here that I think I need to have."

"Well, let's take a look then," she says with a broad smile.

Yes, we're about to make her day.

Two hours and thousands of dollars later, we're walking to the car, loaded down with bags and smiles.

"We shouldn't leave these in the car while we walk to the market," Mer says and frowns.

"Definitely not," I agree and click my fob to unlock the doors. The car is small, so fitting all of the bags and boxes in the backseat is a challenge, but they fit.

And I've broken out in a sweat.

"Maybe we should skip the market today," I suggest. "We can always go another day."

"That's true because you're going to be here for *three months.*"

Meredith hurries around the car and launches herself into my arms, holding me tightly.

"Whoa. This is a lot of affection, Mer." But I hug her back, rocking us both side to side. "But I don't hate it."

"I just love you so much, and I'm happy you're here," she gushes. "I love shopping with you, and seeing you whenever I want to."

"It's fun." I kiss her cheek, then slap her ass. "Now, get in the car, and let's go."

"You're such a softie," she says with a laugh and does as she's told, dropping into the passenger seat. We pull out of the parking garage and head to the freeway, back toward Mer's house, which is in the opposite direction of mine.

"I'm sorry you have to drive so far out of your way," she says. "I should have just driven my own car."

"No way, I get to drive this beauty longer." I wink at her and turn on the radio. *Dance With Me* is playing, so I turn up the volume, and we sing as loudly as we can, doing the arm movements to the choreography as I speed down the freeway.

You know you want it

To feel free, to feel the beat

Move that body, boy

Come on and dance with me

"Do you miss it yet?" she asks when the song is over, and I turn down the volume.

"It's only been a few weeks." I bite my cheek, thinking about it. "I miss the actual concerts. I love them."

"I know you do."

"But I don't miss all the travel. Not knowing where I am. That part is tough."

"You should do a residency in Vegas, then the people can come to you."

"I've been approached about it," I admit, and Mer turns to me in absolute shock.

"Shut up."

"No, really. But I turned it down for now. Maybe in a few years."

"Wow, Starla, I'm so proud of you."

"You do know that if I accept, you and Jax have to come and choreograph the whole fucking show."

She pauses, thinking it over. "That would be a huge undertaking."

"You'd be up for it."

"Damn right, I would be." She grins in excitement. "Just name the place and time, and I'm there."

"I'll keep you posted."

"Now, speaking of keeping me posted, you need to tell me whatever you were mysterious about earlier."

"Oh, right." I clear my throat and change lanes. "I saw Levi yesterday."

"WHAT?" Mer's voice is so shrill when she's excited and surprised at the same time. "This is *not* something you wait until the next day to tell me. It's something you call me about as soon as it's over."

"I'm sorry, I must have missed that memo." I roll my eyes. "Besides, it was just dinner."

"Details, friend. I need details."

"So, he showed up at my place yesterday afternoon. He said he'd been at his brother's house."

"Oh, right! Wyatt lives across the street. That's how he met Lia."

"You could have warned me."

"I forgot." She shrugs. "Keep talking."

"We had a nice conversation, and then when he was leaving,

he told me he'd pick me up for dinner at seven. I didn't argue."

"Oh, God, this is getting good."

"He took me to Red Mill."

"Did you love it?"

"So fucking good, and I'm kind of pissed at you for not taking me there before. Anyway, we had dinner, then we strolled along Alki on the waterfront before he walked me home and kissed me at the front door."

"Holy shit, Star."

"What?"

"You went on a first date."

I pull off the freeway toward Meredith's house.

"I apologized to him for not replying to his texts before."

"Good. Why didn't you?"

I glance over at her. "Duh. Because he overwhelmed me, and after Rick, I was all up in my head about it."

"Well, for what it's worth, I think Levi's fantastic. Also, he's hot."

"So hot." I laugh as I park in her driveway. "You don't even know how hot he is."

"Then I say go for it. You only live once. Rick wouldn't want you to be a nun."

That's exactly what Rick would want.

But I don't say anything. I just shrug, then get out of the car and help her retrieve her bags.

Mark comes out of the house, looking handsome in his shorts and T-shirt.

"Did you buy out the whole store?" he asks as he takes the bags out of my hands, then leans in and kisses his wife.

"We wish," Mer replies with a laugh. "But we did our share."

"Would you like to come in?" Mark asks me.

"No, thanks, I'm going home to put my pretty new things away and maybe take a swim. If I'm feeling extra sassy, I might just take a nap, as well."

"Oh, that sounds so good," Mer says with a sigh. "But I have babies."

"I've got the babies," Mark says with a soft smile. "You nap, M."

"You're both too sweet. I can't watch." I wave and get back in the car, then drive away, headed back toward downtown and the house I'm staying in by the water.

Seattle is beautiful in the summer. I never feel like I'm here long enough to really enjoy it, but I'm here now, and I can honestly say I love it.

I check my phone at a stoplight to make sure I haven't missed any calls or texts, but the phone is quiet, and the screen is blank, which makes me smile.

On a normal day, it would be going crazy.

There might be something to this vacation stuff.

The drive across town doesn't take as long as it normally would, thanks to it being just before rush hour. I'm home in twenty minutes.

Hauling my things inside takes two trips, but I don't mind. I take everything to the spare bedroom where I can unbox my goodies on the bed and leave them there until I decide where I want to store everything.

"That's for later," I decide and announce out loud, hands on my hips. "I think I want a swim."

Thanks to the privacy of the backyard, I don't even have to change into a suit. I just shed my clothes poolside, then dive in and swim until my arms feel like rubber. Even then I don't hop out right away. I float on my back, unconcerned about my breasts being exposed to the sunshine.

I'm a southern girl. I'm used to the sun.

The water feels amazing against my skin and in my hair. It's cooling and calming, making me feel amazing.

I have to admit, since I've been settled in the house, I haven't had many dizzy spells. Maybe the doctor was right, I needed some R&R.

It's been easier than I thought it would be. I'm not bored. If anything, I could use a quiet day with no visitors, just me and my music.

I had Donald send my piano up, and it should arrive this week. I feel the music inside me, ready to come out.

When my eyes get heavy, and I'm worried I'll fall asleep right in the water, I decide it's time to get out.

Once I'm dry, I pad through the house and up the stairs to my bed. For the first time in a *long* time, I'm ready for sleep.

I fall onto the bed, face down, and immediately sink into a deep slumber.

⁓

"YOU LIKE THAT, sweetheart?"

Levi's voice is in my ear, his hands roaming all over my skin, and I'm so turned on, I might come without him even touching my pussy.

"Answer me."

"Yes, I like it. You know I do."

"I love this spot, right here." He kisses my shoulder where it meets my neck. "So soft."

My nipples are hard, painfully so, as he rubs his fingertips over them, plucking them.

"Suck them," I plead, but he shakes his head.

"Not yet."

"Levi, just suck them."

He obliges, latching on, and my body bows off the bed, tightening and straining in reaction to his hot mouth.

"I can't get enough of you," he growls as he plunges inside, fucking me relentlessly until I'm screaming and holding on for dear life.

I wake up and look around, shocked to find that I'm alone, in my bed, with the sun setting, casting the room in shadows.

My naked body is on *fire*. I'm panting. My legs scissor, desperate to release the tension in my core.

My hand drifts down my belly, over my smooth pubis, and my fingers make contact with my hard, throbbing clit.

I'd rather it was Levi, but he's not here, so I do what I need to in order to relieve my frustration. Thinking of Levi's mischievous smile and the way his voice sounds in my ear as he urges me toward climax is all it takes to send me over the edge.

I sigh, brush my still-damp hair off my cheek, and reach for my phone in case I've missed anything.

Shit, it's past seven.

And I've missed two texts from Levi.

Hey gorgeous. I hope you had a great day.

That was two hours ago. There's another.

I'd like to swing by and see you. Please let me know if you'd rather I didn't.

That was thirty minutes ago.

I'm about to reply when the doorbell rings. I sit up on the

bed, eyes wide, heart hammering.

"Damn it." I stub my toe as I search for my shorts. "Fuck, that hurts."

I hop around, into the shorts and a tank, not bothering with underwear, and hurry down the stairs.

The house is dark when I open the door and find a grinning Levi in my doorway.

"You didn't say *not* to come over." His eyes narrow as he looks me up and down. "You were sleeping."

"I just woke up a few minutes ago." I swallow and push my hair back. I hope my rosy cheeks don't give away the fact that I just came to thoughts of him not even five minutes ago. "Come on in."

"I'm sorry, Star—"

"No, it's okay," I assure him as he steps inside, and I flip on a light. "I slept way too long. I never nap. Must have been the shopping and the sex. I mean, the swim."

I shake my head and laugh as his head whips my way, and he glares.

"Back it up."

"There was no sex." I'm laughing now, belly laughs that I can't control. "At least, not with another person."

"Fuck." It's a mumble as he rubs his fingers over his mouth. "I don't know if I want to know."

I'm feeling fresh and sassy, so I boost myself up to sit on the kitchen counter and kick my feet back and forth.

"I went shopping with Meredith. Did a bit of damage that I have zero regrets about. Then I came back here and took a long swim. It made me sleepy, so I took a nap."

"And then?" His dark eyes are on fire as he slowly advances

on me, each step bringing him closer.

"I had a dream about you," I whisper, watching every move he makes. "And when I woke up, I worked myself to orgasm."

He's standing directly in front of me now, but not touching me.

"While thinking of me."

"Yes."

He sighs and reaches out to tuck my hair behind my ear.

"That might be the sexiest thing anyone has ever said to me."

I cock an eyebrow. "Ever?"

"Ever."

I want him closer. I want him to step between my legs, rip my tiny shorts in half, and have his way with me right here in the kitchen.

"You're thinking dangerous thoughts," he murmurs.

"Oh, yeah," I agree with a slow nod. "Lots of them. But something tells me fucking me here on the counter isn't in your plans."

He hangs his head, a stream of swear words coming out of his sexy mouth, and it makes me laugh. When he looks at me again, his face is taut with strain and regret.

"I promised myself I wouldn't take it there for a while. I want us to get to know each other better before we go to bed together."

"Good plan." I nod as if it makes total sense. "Of course, having sex is just another way to get to know each other. And I promise I'll text you in the morning, so you don't feel . . ."

"Feel what?"

"Cheap? Unwanted? Dismissed?"

"I did feel all of those things."

I cup his cheek and urge him closer.

"You're *none* of those things, Levi, and I deeply regret making you feel that way. It won't happen again."

His hand mirrors mine. He cups my cheek and rubs his thumb back and forth.

"Starla."

"Yes."

"What are you wearing under these ridiculous excuses for clothes?"

A naughty smile flirts over my lips. "Absolutely nothing."

"Fuck."

four

Starla

He steps closer, closing the small gap between us, and kisses my forehead then down my nose and over to each cheek. The kisses are light and soft and lull me back into a sweet haze of lust.

I purr. That's the only way to describe it. It's not a moan or a groan. It's a freaking purr, and Levi is the only person in my life who's ever made that noise come from my body.

"You smell amazing," he whispers as he kisses my earlobe and then just below it on the soft skin of my neck. "And I love this spot, right here."

It's just like my dream. Levi places a wet kiss on my neck, then tugs the skin between his teeth, not biting hard enough to leave a mark.

Not that he's above that. I had bite marks on my ass for a week after our night together weeks ago.

It was fantastic.

I drag my foot up the back of his leg, urging him closer. My skin is on fire, wanting nothing more than for us to be naked together, moving in harmony. I can hear the music of the sex we have together in my head, and it's heady.

Intoxicating.

"Jesus, you'd tempt a saint," he murmurs, tugging the strap of my tank down my arm, exposing the top of my breast. "Your skin is so damn soft."

I bury my fingers in his hair, delighted when he kisses lower, exposing my bare breast and pulling the hard nipple into his mouth.

"Yes," I cry, enthralled by the way he feels against me. There's a little stubble on his face, leaving a light burn on my skin. His finger pushes the fabric of my denim shorts aside and plunges inside me, sending sparks shooting through my whole body. My legs lock around his thighs, and he grins against me before looking up into my eyes.

"You're so damn wet," he says.

"Shocking," I say, then gasp when he adds another finger. "Oh, Lord, that's good."

"So tight." He eases me closer to the edge of the countertop but holds me steady so I can't fall. "I need more access to you."

"You can have all the access you want."

With two fingers still inside me, he presses the heel of his hand against my clit. And that's all I can take. I fly over the edge of insanity, soaring high as the orgasm consumes me, shattering me completely.

He peppers my skin with kisses, crooning soft words that I can't make out over the rushing in my ears, but it feels damn good.

Maybe better than I've ever felt in my whole life.

"Better?" he asks.

"Whoa," is all I can say.

"Are you steady?"

I frown up at him. "Yeah."

"Good."

He turns away from me to wash his hands in the sink, and I'm confused.

"We're done?"

He sends a glance my way over his shoulder but finishes washing up without a word. Finally, while he wipes his hands dry, he turns and leans his hips against the counter opposite of me.

"I think we are, yes."

"But you didn't—"

"I'm fine," he says but then cringes. "Okay, I'm not *fine*. But I'll live."

I feel completely rejected. Embarrassed. No, *mortified* is a better word.

"Listen, I'm sorry that I threw myself at you, and you felt like you needed to give me a pity orgasm."

I hop off the counter and hurry past him toward the living room.

"You don't have to stay—"

"Stop."

I don't turn around. He's standing behind me, and his voice is hard, but I can't turn around and look him in the eyes because I'm *so fucking embarrassed*.

"Look at me."

"I'd rather not."

"Shit." He hurries around me and takes my hands in his, kissing them both. "Look at me, Starla."

I finally look up, and he has remorse written all over his handsome face.

"If you weren't into it, you should have said so," I say at last, not willing to back down from this.

"Not into it?" He scowls and pulls my hand down to his crotch, pressing my palm against the hard-on he's sporting behind his jeans. "If I was any *more* into it, I'd be busting out of my pants for God's sake."

"Then why?"

He blows out a breath. "Okay, I'm going to be brutally honest here."

He hated the sex. He never wants to have sex with me again. I'm an idiot.

"I want nothing more than to be buried so deep inside of you right now that I don't know where I end and you begin."

"Awesome."

"But, I also want to go slow. I'm not trying to hurt you here, Starla, but you have this incredible, unexpected power over me, and I have to be careful around you. You *did* hurt me before. And I know you've apologized. I'm not holding that over your head."

"It feels like it," I admit.

"I'm sorry." He kisses my forehead. "I'm trying to be a gentleman here, damn it."

I smile. "Well, that's nice of you."

"I'm a nice guy." His voice is light as if he's teasing, but it's the truth. He *is* a nice guy. "So, we're going to date for a while before we go back to the sex part."

"I can't," I say. "I can't date like a normal person, Levi."

"Why the hell not?"

"Hello. Look at me." I wave my hand over my face and stomp away in frustration.

"You're gorgeous."

"I'm *Starla*."

"Yes, you are."

"You're being difficult." I scratch my hands through my hair in frustration.

"I'm not trying to be. Obviously, I'm missing something here."

"I'm too famous to date, and that's not me trying to be a diva. It's just the truth. I have to wear a disguise when I leave the house because, otherwise, I'll be mobbed."

"Look, I'm not here because you're *Starla*. I don't care."

"If I thought otherwise, you wouldn't be standing in my living room with my come on your hands."

He narrows his eyes. "Watch yourself."

I narrow my eyes back at him and walk closer. "Or what?"

"I may not be willing to fuck you right now, but I'll spank that gorgeous ass of yours. Where have you always wanted to go in Seattle that you can't?"

I stop short, halted by both the question and the ass-spanking comment.

I honestly wouldn't mind if he spanked me.

"Focus," he says with a smirk.

"The Pop Culture Museum," I reply immediately. "I've heard the Nirvana and Kurt Cobain exhibit is amazing, but there's no way I can go in there."

"Because you're Starla."

"They've asked to use some of my memorabilia in the museum, Levi. If I walk in there during business hours, I'd have a mob on my hands."

He nods and retrieves his phone from his back pocket.

"Go get dressed."

"Where are we going?"

He sighs and stares at me in frustration. "Can't a man surprise you just a little? I'm sweeping you off your feet here. Go get dressed."

I grin, suddenly excited to see what he's got up his sleeve. Before I rush upstairs to get dressed, I leap into his arms and plant my lips against his, kissing him fast and furiously before jumping down and hurrying to change my clothes.

"I'll be down in ten minutes!"

"I'll be here."

"IT'S CLOSED," I say when we walk up to the Pop Culture Museum doors. It's near the base of the Space Needle, in the heart of downtown. The sun has long been down, but people are bustling about, enjoying the warm summer evening.

At least with the sun down, the likelihood of being recognized is lessened.

"Don't worry," he says, smiling down at me and squeezing my hand.

A man appears at the door and unlocks it for us, then locks us in.

"Hey, Levi," he says, holding his hand out to shake.

"Luke," Levi says with a nod.

"Hey, Starla," Luke says with a smile, and I immediately walk into his arms for a warm hug.

"I didn't know you'd be meeting us here." I step back and smile up at the ridiculously handsome man. He's married to Natalie, the woman who owns the house I'm staying in, and he's one of Hollywood's hottest movie producers.

Not to mention, back in the day, he was one of the most famous movie stars there was.

"It was a surprise," he says with a laugh. "When Levi called and asked me to get you guys in here, I was happy to oblige. I've had the staff turn on all of the lights throughout all of the exhibits, so feel free to look around at everything."

"What, do you own the joint?" I ask with a laugh.

"No, it's a non-profit," Levi says.

"But I've made sizeable contributions, and I know the people in charge." Luke winks. "I'll leave you to it. Ralph, the evening janitor, is around to turn off the lights and lock the door behind you when you're done."

"Thanks, man," Levi says.

"My pleasure. Enjoy." He turns to walk away but stops short. "Oh, two more things. Natalie told me to tell you both to come over for dinner tomorrow. She'll text you the time. And the Nirvana exhibit is down that way."

"Thanks." I grin at him and almost melt into a puddle when he winks at me before walking away.

"Do you have a crush on Luke?"

"Don't *you* have a crush on Luke?" I counter as we walk down to the Nirvana exhibit. "He's ridiculously handsome."

"I'm going to have to kill him," Levi mutters, making me laugh.

"Nah." I boost up on my toes to kiss his cheek. "He's happily married, and I can't seem to stop thinking about you, so we're good. Oh, my God."

I stop cold in the doorway and just look around the room. An interview is playing through the speakers, Kurt's voice talking about their start in Aberdeen, Washington.

"Look at these photos," I whisper, pouring over Polaroids in a glass case. The whole band in the late '80s is in the photos, young and acting silly. Their eyes are full of cockiness and humor. Hope. Love.

We spend an hour, reading journals and postcards, watching interviews, and I long to reach through the glass to play Kurt's guitar.

"I met Dave Grohl," I say as we walk out of the room toward an exhibit about *Star Trek*. "A couple of times, actually. But at one event in particular, I was able to sit with him and talk about music, how it's changed over the past thirty years, and thank him for inspiring me as a young woman."

"That must have been amazing."

I glance up and smile. "It was the best moment of my life. There are so many musicians that I admire, that inspire me, but Nirvana was special."

"You were young when they were popular."

"Very." I nod thoughtfully. "And I couldn't get enough of them. Their songs inspired me to write my own."

"Fascinating," Levi says. "Your music is so different from theirs."

"You listen to my music?"

"Of course, I do," he replies with a shrug. "It's all over the radio."

"Give me your phone." I stop in the middle of the Marvel exhibit, right in front of Iron Man, holding out my hand.

"Why?"

"I want to see something."

He unlocks his phone and passes it to me, and I immediately open his music app, search my name, and feel my eyes go wide when I see every song I've ever released on his device.

"Levi."

"I guess you've poured some of your heart out, so I should do the same."

He takes his phone back, stuffs it into his back pocket, and holds my hand as we wander around. "I had only heard the music on the radio before our first night together, and if you remember correctly, earlier that day when Jace, Joy, and I all met you at Meredith and Mark's house, I didn't recognize who you were."

"Oh, yeah," I say, laughing at the memory. "Joy was mortified that you guys didn't know me, but it was actually really refreshing."

"I'd heard your music, but no, I didn't know who you were. After our night together, I downloaded everything I could find."

"Why?"

"Because I felt closer to you while I was listening to the music, the lyrics. Getting to know you, I guess."

Levi's not wrong. I pour *everything* into my music.

"You're a sweet man." I kiss his shoulder. "And I have so many regrets about the days after we were together."

"Let's not dwell on regrets," he says as we make our way through the last exhibit, about '80s movies. "Let's just move on from here. I'm just happy to spend time with you, sweetheart. We'll take it slow."

"Maybe we'll call it *going at our own pace*, rather than *taking it slow.*" I grin up at him and sigh when he pulls me to him and kisses me with a passion I haven't known in five years. I didn't think I'd ever feel it again, and yet here it is.

I'm enjoying it, and I'm scared of it.

I'm just not willing to let it go.

I'VE DECIDED I'M addicted to swimming. Until my piano gets here, I need a creative outlet, and it seems that means I'm in the water.

It's mid-morning. I slept like the dead last night and woke up feeling feisty and ready to go. The best part?

No dizziness. None.

It's amazing how good I feel.

I'm paddling backward, enjoying the way the sunshine feels on my face and listening to the birds singing in the trees. I should use my pool more often in LA. If I were home more.

When I reach the end of the pool, I flip over and do the breaststroke to the other side, then turn onto my back and mosey back the way I came.

All in all, it's not a bad way to spend the morning.

After a few more laps, I stand to walk out of the pool.

"Fuck!" I scream, clutching my chest over my pounding heart at the sight of Levi lounging lazily in a pool chair. "How long have you been here?"

"Long enough to count ten laps," he says with a smile. "If I'd known you swam naked, I would have come by earlier."

"Funny." I don't bother to cover my nakedness as I walk into the house to the bathroom where I have towels and fresh clothes waiting for me.

"You've got a great backstroke," he says from the doorway, grinning like a fool.

"I'm glad you got a good show." I laugh as I tie my wet hair up in the towel and reach for my underwear. "What are you doing here, anyway?"

"I brought coffee."

"I don't drink coffee."

"I remember." He sips from his to-go mug, smiling at me over the rim. "But I wanted coffee."

"Do they not sell coffee by your house?"

"Where do you think I got this?"

I tilt my head, watching him. "None of this makes sense."

"I wanted to drink my coffee while I sat with you."

"Huh." I unwrap the towel and comb my tangled hair, then twist it into a wet knot. "Well, looks like you managed to pull that off."

"I sure did." He chuckles. I should be mad at him for watching me when I didn't know that he was there, but I'm not. At all. He's already seen me. And I like having him nearby. "I thought I'd pick you up to go to Nat and Luke's for dinner, too."

"We don't have to be there for about seven hours."

"Oh, good. We have time then."

"You're so mysterious today. Time for what?"

"You'll see."

five

Levi

"I'm not dressed to go anywhere," Starla says in protest as I lead her by the hand out her front door. "Seriously, I'm a mess."

"We're not going far," I assure her. We walk past our cars and across the street to Wyatt and Lia's house.

"I'm definitely not looking good enough to see your family right now."

I stop in the middle of the road and tug her to me. God, she molds against me like she was fucking made for me.

"You would look good with the damn plague, Starla. Just trust me here, okay?"

Her eyes roam my face, and finally, she nods once. "Okay."

I kiss her forehead before setting off again, moving up Wyatt's driveway to ring the doorbell.

"You're here!" Lia exclaims when she opens the door.

"Lia, this is Starla," I say lamely as Lia takes my girl's hand and happily leads her into the house.

"Duh," she says with a laugh. "I didn't get to meet you when you were in town for the show because Wyatt and I were on our honeymoon, but I heard it was *ridiculously* amazing."

"Thank you," Starla says with a smile. "Meredith has told me a bit about you guys."

"What, my loving brother-in-law hasn't been singing my praises?" Lia props her hands on her hips and glares at me. "Just kidding."

"Hi, Starla," Wyatt says as he holds his hand out to shake hers. "Welcome."

"Thank you," Starla replies again. "I'm happy to meet you both, I'm just a little—"

She looks at me for help, but before I can say anything, Lia jumps in.

"Confused as to why you're here," Lia guesses. "Levi called me this morning and explained that he would like to date you properly, which I kind of swooned over if I'm being honest."

Starla blinks rapidly, still staring at me, and her plump lips part in surprise.

"And he told me about your challenges with being recognized in public, which I can completely understand. I don't have even a fraction of the celebrity you do, and I'm recognized sometimes, too. Not to mention, my cousin is married to Luke Williams, and we have Will Montgomery and Leo Nash in the family."

"That's one intimidating family," Starla says. "Every time I go to a family function with you guys, it's like being at the Grammys and the Oscars at the same time."

"I know," Lia says with a laugh. "And I'm not rattling all of that off to show off, but to say that I understand your need for privacy and to just go to the grocery store without it being an event."

"Exactly." Starla relaxes immensely, and the smile she gives Lia is genuine. This was *not* a bad idea.

Thank Christ.

"I'm a makeup lover," Lia continues as she leads Starla to the dining room table that's covered from end to end with tubes and brushes and more color than the human eye should be able to take in. "I have my own line coming in a few months."

"I heard," Starla says, startling Lia. "I can't wait to try it."

"Oh, hold please."

Lia rushes out of the room, running quickly for a girl in bare feet, then returns holding a big, pink shopping bag.

"You can have everything."

"Holy shit," Starla says, peeking into the bag. "This is *incredible*. Thank you so much. I'll share on my social media."

The room is silent as Wyatt and I just watch our girls interact. Without a word, my brother passes me a bottle of water. We're fascinated.

Lia just blinks at Starla, then suddenly, her eyes fill with tears.

"Oh my gosh," she whispers.

"If you don't want me to share, I won't," Starla quickly says, but Lia shakes her head adamantly as she dabs at the tears.

"You have no idea how that could help me," she says, her voice thick. "It could be a game changer."

"I have a feeling I'll be paying you back for whatever it is we're about to do."

"Oh!" Lia laughs and looks over at Wyatt with shiny blue eyes as she pulls her thoughts together. "Focus. Okay, we're going to give you a disguise."

Starla scowls. "I can do that on my own. I just wear a hat

and some sunglasses. Sometimes, I'll throw on a wig."

"Too obvious," Lia says, shaking her head. "You look like someone in disguise. The whole purpose of a disguise is to blend. To make others think you're someone else. I've got some wigs here that I picked up, and I'm going to show you how to do your makeup and wear the hair so you don't look like Starla anymore, but just the girl next door going on a date with your boyfriend."

"He's not—"

"Doesn't matter," Lia says with a flick of the wrist, and I can't help but smile at my brother, who's also chuckling. I bet Starla doesn't have many people in her life that just take over.

It's fun to watch.

"Blond or brunette?" Lia asks her. "The hair color will affect the makeup."

Starla glances at me. "Do you have a preference?"

"Plague," I repeat, making her laugh. "You choose."

"Let's go brunette. I haven't done that in more than a decade."

"Brunette it is," Lia says with glee. "Oh my God, this is so fun. Now, this is how you apply the wig so it doesn't *look* like a wig."

"It's a good thing you're across the street," Starla says dubiously. "I have a feeling this is going to include a steep learning curve."

"I've got you, friend. Now, hold it like this . . ."

"I CAN'T BELIEVE it," Starla says an hour later as we sit in my vehicle, driving toward downtown Seattle. "I look so *different.*"

"It's amazing," I agree as I glance her way. The brunette wig is short, just hitting her collarbones. It has bangs, but the hair looks natural.

Lia applied the makeup with a light hand while changing Starla's features just enough that a person might say, *"you look like . . ."* but not believe that she's *actually* Starla.

"Lia's one talented woman," Starla says as she tucks the mirror away and relaxes in the seat. "Where are we going?"

"Have you been to Pike's Place Market?"

"No, I was supposed to go there a few days ago with Mer, but we got sidetracked buying out Chanel. I've always wanted to see it."

"I thought we'd roam around the market for a while, and then the Space Needle, unless you've done that before and you'd rather do something else."

"Never done it," she confirms with a firm shake of the head. "I've only seen the outside."

"Well then, you're about to be a tourist, beautiful lady."

She smiles with excitement. "Wait. You have to call me Beth today. To go with the disguise."

"That might be hard to remember. What if you don't respond to it when I call for you?"

"I will. It's my real name." She says it like it's no big deal, but this is news to me.

"Seriously?"

"Yeah. Beth Anne March. That's my given name."

"Huh. How did you come up with Starla?"

"I read it in a book when I was a kid and liked it." She shrugs. "So, when I moved to LA to pursue the music, I changed it legally. On paper, I'm Starla Mason."

"Where is your family?"

She frowns but doesn't answer, and I can feel by the shift in the air that this isn't a subject she wants to talk about. I'm a cop. I know when someone's evading or dodging. I would normally let it go, but I'm falling in love with this woman, and I want to know *everything* there is to know about her.

"If you don't want to talk about it today, that's fine," I say and feel her sigh in relief. "But we'll come back to it. I want to know everything there is to know, the good and the bad."

"That's fair," she says and clears her throat. "I'm having a great day, and I'd like to keep it that way, so do you mind if we shelve this for now?"

"No. I don't mind." I take her hand in mine and kiss her knuckles just before I pull into a parking garage. I find a spot, hurry around the car to open Starla's door, then lace her fingers with mine and lead her down the steep hill to the market below."

"Wait, I have to take a picture of this." She stops me halfway down the hill and snaps a photo of the iconic Market sign with the Sound in the background.

"Alki is right over there." I point straight ahead at the beach across from us.

"Wow, it looks so far away." She sniffs the air. "Do I smell donuts?"

"You have the nose of a bloodhound."

"I do when it comes to donuts," she agrees. "And Mer told me about tiny donuts to die for."

"They aren't just a legend." I wrap my arm around her shoulders and kiss the top of her wig as she loops her arm around my waist. "I'll buy you all the donuts you want, babe."

"Nice." She smiles up at me. "Do we get to see flying fish, too?"

"You already know a lot about the market."

"Yes, and now I get to see it." She gives me a squeeze. "Thank you. For all of this. For all of today."

"You're welcome."

The tiny donuts are a hit. She has to try some of every flavor, so we order three dozen of the little treats. I don't complain; between the two of us, they'll be gone before we leave here today.

"Holy shit," she mutters, her mouth full of cinnamon and sugar deliciousness. "So damn good."

"They're my favorite."

"I have to go dance with Jax tomorrow," she says before taking another bite. "If I don't, I'll gain twenty pounds."

"I think you'll be okay." We wander the short distance to where the fish throwers put on a show, and we're not disappointed as a salmon goes flying through the air. We stand, eat, and watch until the crowd thins out a bit, then we walk on. Street musicians fill the air with songs, and we're met with the scent of flowers and vegetables as we make our way farther into the covered market, weaving our way through the crowd.

"Oh my God, look that these." Starla leans down to smell a bunch of flowers and smiles happily. "I'll take two."

"Two?"

"One for me, and one for Lia. She earned them."

Starla's kind-hearted. The more I'm with her, the more pulled to her I am. My dick is constantly at half-mast, and the slightest touch, the barest glance can set my body on fire.

But more than that, I'm entranced by her sweet nature. Her humor. Her intelligence. Being with Starla is no hardship.

We gather the flowers, pick through the produce to find some favorites, and then make our way back to the car.

"This was *incredible*."

"I'm glad you liked it. We can come back anytime."

"No one looked twice at me," she continues. "No side-eyes, no gropes."

"Wait. People *grope* you?"

"All the time." She shrugs as if it's no big thing, but I'm *pissed*.

"Why don't you have security with you all the time?"

She rolls her eyes. "Now you sound like Donald."

"Who the fuck is Donald?"

"My manager." She frowns up at me. "I don't have constant security because I'm a human being who wants to live a normal life."

We get to the car, and I stow our things in the backseat before sitting next to her and slamming the door.

"I understand how normalcy would be important, but you're also a megastar, and there are real challenges that come with that."

"If you think I'm not aware of that—"

"I know you are, I just think you should have better security."

"Thank you." Her voice is calm, surprising me. "Thank you for caring enough about me to worry. It means more than you know."

She takes my hand and presses it against her cheek before kissing my palm. I went from DEFCON 6 to calm in three seconds.

She's amazing.

"I'm always careful. And now I have magic makeup powers

to help disguise myself when I want to go to the market with my *boyfriend.*"

She's smirking, but her eyes are serious as she watches for my reaction.

I lean over and press my lips to hers, softly. Sweetly.

"I'll never let anything happen to you," I promise. "Ever."

"I know."

"AND THEN WE went to the Space Needle." Starla's standing next to Natalie in the kitchen, sampling the yellow peppers from the salad. "And we could see *forever.*"

"The view up there is incredible," Natalie agrees with a grin. She's stirring something on the stove. Luke walks up behind her and kisses her neck, then walks away. "I bet you could see all the way to Oregon on a beautiful day like today."

"I bet you're right," Starla says with a serious nod. "And the best part?"

"Let me guess," Luke says as he takes a seat next to me at the bar. "No one recognized you."

"Not *one* person," Starla says before doing a little shimmy right there in the kitchen.

Jesus, I want to boost her up onto the countertop and feast on *her* for dinner.

"Lia's *so* good," Nat says. "Seriously, if I didn't already know you, I don't think I could have picked you out of a lineup."

"It's amazing because what she did was so subtle. It's all about contouring and shading." Starla takes another bite of pepper. "How do you deal with the attention, Luke?"

Luke frowns and takes a sip from his glass of beer. "I didn't deal well, let me tell you."

"That's how we met," Nat says with a laugh. "He assaulted me on Alki Beach."

"Would you *please* stop telling people that?"

"No way." Nat sets her spoon aside and turns to Starla. "I was taking photos one morning . . . *not* of him—"

"It looked like the lens was pointed at me."

"—and suddenly he rips my camera away from me and threatens to kill me if I don't delete the photos."

"You're getting a spanking," Luke says with a sigh. "I never threatened to kill you."

"Okay, but he threatened legal action. And he tried to steal my camera."

"I've never heard this story," I say with a laugh, picturing it in my head. "This could be the best how-did-you-meet story I've ever heard."

"I had to flip through the photos to prove to him that he wasn't on there. He's a little full of himself."

"Natalie," Luke warns, making his wife giggle.

"Actually, in all seriousness, Luke had a lot of anxiety about being recognized. That's why he was pissed when he saw me taking the photos. He thought I was the press."

"I get it," Starla says with a nod. "It sucks. I would think it's better in Seattle than LA, though."

"It is," Luke confirms. "But it still happens, especially back then when the *Nightwalker* movies were still fresh in everyone's mind."

"I freaking *loved* those movies," Starla says with an excited smile. "You were a hot vampire."

Luke squirms in his seat, making Natalie laugh.

"Anyway, I didn't recognize him," Nat says. "I had no idea who this nut job was, aside from a handsome weirdo."

"Darling, you cut me to the core."

Nat waves him off.

"Have you ever done the disguise thing?" I ask him.

"No. I just became a recluse. And as time goes on, I'm recognized less. Or, people just leave me alone."

"It helps that he's behind the camera now instead of in front of it," Nat adds.

"Unless I want to be a songwriter and not the singer, I don't have that luxury," Starla says with a sigh. "And I don't mean to sound like I'm complaining. I'm not. I have a crazy, luxurious life."

"We understand," Nat says with a supportive pat to Starla's back. "You're not ungrateful. You're cautious. Because whether you like it or not, you've traded a good portion of your privacy for celebrity. And even with all of the benefits, there are some pitfalls."

"Some of them can be scary," Luke adds. "But you're a smart woman, Star, and you've been doing this a long time."

"Yeah." She sighs, and I can tell that something is running through her gorgeous brain.

"What is it?" I ask.

"I wonder how a person knows when it's time to slow down."

"That's up to you," Nat replies. "Leo didn't start to slow down until this year after Sam finally drew a line in the sand. She wants the luxury of living with her husband. But she also understands that the job is important to him."

"Will's in the same boat," Luke adds. "I think there comes a time for everyone when they start to really think about what's most important. And it's okay if those things change over time."

"Boy," Starla says with a sigh. "This is a *deep* conversation. But thanks for listening. I guess I needed to talk to someone else who gets it, you know?"

"Oh, I get it," Luke assures her. "And I'm always here, just up the street, if you want to talk about it more."

"Thanks. Hey, don't you have a million kids? Where are they?"

"At Luke's parents," Nat says. "Trust me, it's better this way."

"I like kids," Starla says but won't meet my eyes. "But this is good, too."

"I'm starving." I change the subject on purpose. It's time to lighten things up around here. But when I have Starla to myself, I have a list of questions for her.

"Dinner's ready," Nat says. "Let's eat."

six

Levi

"Feed her."

Joy, my brother Jace's wife, gently places a tiny kitten in my hands then gives me a little bottle of milk.

"Uh, Joy, I'm not really—"

"If you want breakfast, you'll feed her," she says as she walks away and whisks the eggs.

It's the morning after my day out with Starla. I haven't seen Jace in a couple of weeks thanks to both of our schedules, and I'm happy to spend time with him and Joy, catching up.

I brush my thumb along the top of the kitten's head and offer her the nipple, which she latches on to right away.

"Do you ever feed her?"

"Every two hours," Joy confirms. "You should adopt her once she's ready to go home."

"No." I shake my head adamantly. "No pets for me."

"I'll talk you into it eventually." Joy's voice is confident. She may be right, but I'll continue putting up a fight.

Mostly because it's fun.

"So, what have you been up to?" Joy asks, her voice way too nonchalant for me to believe she doesn't already know what I've been doing.

"Who have you talked to?"

"I don't know what you mean."

"Bullshit."

She laughs, and I stare at Jace, who just shrugs and takes another sip of his coffee, watching his wife with the proverbial heart eyes.

"There might be a rumor floating through the family that you're dating Starla."

"And you're looking for confirmation?"

"Yes." She stirs the eggs in the pan and smiles over at me. "So, what have you been up to?"

"Nothing." I laugh when she scowls.

"Watching you two banter is exhausting," Jace says.

"It's your fault, dude. You started bringing her around fifteen years ago, and she's been a pain in my ass ever since."

"Hey," Joy demands. "You love me, and you know it."

"I can love you and still find you to be a pain in my ass." The kitten is making a mess of the milk, so I set the bottle down and use a paper towel to clean her up. "Is she done?"

Joy shrugs because she knows my pain in the ass statement is true, and once she has our plates loaded with eggs and bacon, she sets them in front of us, then takes the kitten from me and tucks her into a warm blanket.

"She's done. And I have toast coming." Joy says.

"This is way more than I expected when I said I was coming over."

"You've got to eat," she replies. "And, if you're not dating Starla, which as you pointed out is none of my business, I have a new doctor at my clinic I'd like to introduce you to. MaryLou. She's super smart and funny. Right, Jace?"

"Sure," he says, shoving eggs in his pie-hole.

"Whose side are you on?" I ask him, earning an eye roll.

"I have sex with *her*," he reminds me. "Whose side do you think I'm on?"

"Anyway, MaryLou is super sweet, and I think you'd hit it off." I glare at my sister-in-law and, in my head, run through all the ways I could kill her and make it look like an accident before she follows up with, "I just want you to be happy, Levi. I love you."

Okay, there will be no killing today.

"Are you going to control your woman?" I ask my brother.

"Nope."

I sigh and take a bite of toast. "I've been seeing Starla."

"I *knew* it!" Joy pumps her fist in victory. "Tell me everything. Not just your cop version of the events, which is never enough. *Everything*, Crawford."

"You're truly a pain in my ass."

"Go on. Spill it."

I look helplessly at Jace, but he just shrugs.

"It's not the job giving me the grey hair, it's my nosy-ass sisters-in-law."

Joy just watches me expectantly, and finally, I cave.

"It's really pretty normal dating stuff."

"Like?"

"I took her out to dinner, to the Pop Culture Museum, the Market. You know, the usual."

"Without being mobbed?"

"Lia helped." I tell them about Lia giving Starla a disguise. "It was fun to take her out where she could relax and enjoy herself."

"That's *so* awesome," Joy says. "She seems really nice."

"She is."

"So that's it?"

"That's it." I shove more food into my mouth and chew, holding Joy's gaze with my own in a stare-down of wits.

"I don't believe you."

"What else do you want to know?"

"Are you sleeping with her?"

"Jesus, Joy."

"I told you, I want to know everything."

"No," I blurt, surprised at myself. "No, I'm not sleeping with her. Not for now."

Jace and Joy both blink at me in surprise.

"Really?" Jace asks first. "Wow."

"What does that mean?"

"Just wow," he says. "From what you told me, the chemistry is crazy hot, so I just figured—"

"Wait," Joy says, holding up a hand. "He told *you* the chemistry is hot? Why didn't you tell *me*?"

"Because some things are private," I say at last and then feel like shit when her eyes have hurt in them. "And because she fucked me up in the head before, and I didn't know how to deal with it. I just needed to talk it out with Jace."

"I can see that," Joy says, the hurt leaving her eyes. "How do you feel?"

"Still a little messed up," I admit. "But I like her, and I want to get to know her better."

"Well, I think it's fantastic," Joy says. "I'll keep MaryLou as a backup, just in case."

"You're a meddler," I say, pointing at her with my toast.

"Thank you for noticing."

"JESUS, WHY DOES the paperwork pile up over the weekend?"

I stare at my inbox, both on my desk and on the computer, and sigh.

"Because everyone missed you, Crawford," Anderson says from the doorway of my office just as my phone rings.

"Crawford."

"This is dispatch. We have a burglary call at 7720 North 77th Street."

"On my way." I stand and reach for my leather jacket. "Paperwork will have to wait. We have a call. You're with me."

"I'm ready," Anderson replies and falls into step behind me. Anderson's a rookie. He's been in my division for less than a year, but I like him. He has strong instincts, and a solid work ethic, which I've found is sorely lacking in the young guys coming through the academy these days.

The drive to the address in question takes ten minutes. When we pull up, there's already a cruiser there with its lights flashing, and the front door of the house is open. Neighbors stand outside and on tiptoe to peek through windows, trying to see what's going on.

I approach, calling out my name and rank.

The patrolman on scene steps to the door.

"A woman named Francesca Smith called it in," he says, quickly briefing me. "She insists that she's missing property but can't tell me exactly what's gone."

"Tape off the perimeter," I instruct him. "I don't want neighbors walking on the property in case we need to look for footprints in the grass."

"Will do."

He nods and steps out, and Anderson and I walk in to find a crying woman on the couch.

"Hello, Miss Smith, I'm Detective Crawford, and this is my partner, Officer Anderson."

"Hello," she whines, sniffing at her tears. "Thank you for coming."

"Can you tell me what happened?"

"Well, like I told the other guy, I woke up and just *knew* someone had been in my house."

"How do you know?" I ask as Anderson takes his phone out of his pocket and starts taking notes. I survey the scene, looking over the windows and doors to the outside.

Aside from the front door, it doesn't appear that anything is open.

"I could *feel* it," she says. "And I know you're going to tell me I'm crazy, but I'm not. I have women's intuition."

"I don't think you're crazy."

Yet.

"Were any of your doors or windows open?"

"No," she says and sniffs again. "But my mother's wedding ring is missing."

This piques my interest.

"Can you describe it?"

"I have a photo of it," she says and brings it up on her phone to show me. "It's a simple gold band."

I look at Anderson, who looks back at me.

"Is it engraved inside?"

"No." She sniffs once more.

"Is anything else missing? Any other jewelry?"

"No. That's why it *has* to be Jeremy that did it."

"Jeremy?" I raise a brow. "You *know* who did this?"

She nods and starts to cry again. "He's obsessed with me. He won't leave me alone."

Anderson and I share another look.

"Is he stalking you?" I ask.

"Absolutely. We work together, and I've told him I don't want to jeopardize my job. I mean, he's cute and all, but it's not worth losing my job over. He just won't take no for an answer, and he knows that ring means a lot to me, so he took it just to hurt me."

I frown. It doesn't make a lot of sense, but it won't hurt to have a conversation with Jeremy.

"Fran, what's Jeremy's last name?"

"My name is *Francesca*," she bites out, glaring at me. "I didn't give you permission to call me *Fran*."

"My apologies." I glance around the room again. "Do you mind if I look around?"

"Why? I told you what I'm missing."

"Someone was in your home without your permission," I remind her, watching her closely. "I'd just like to take a quick look."

"Fine."

She dissolves into another puddle of tears, and I know

Anderson won't like babysitting her, but I leave him with her while I walk the space. The house is small and simply decorated. Nothing fancy. The woman who lives here is tidy but clearly doesn't make a ton of money.

There's nothing here that screams foul play.

When I return to the living area, Francesca is snapping at my partner.

"I saw the way you looked at me."

"I wasn't looking at you, ma'am."

"Now I'm a ma'am?" She stands and pokes her finger into his chest. "I don't like you."

"You don't have to like him," I interrupt, pissed now. "And you'd best not touch him again, or I'll arrest you for assault of a police officer."

"He was *looking* at me."

"He won't be looking anymore. We're done here." I nod at Anderson, and he immediately turns and walks out of the house. "I'll call you if the ring turns up. It would help if you'd tell me Jeremy's last name."

"Lubbock," she says. "Like the city. Please talk to him and tell him to leave me alone."

"I'll talk to him. If you're that afraid of him, you can take out a restraining order."

"I was hoping it wouldn't come to that," she says with a sigh.

I tip my head and leave, closing the door behind me, then walk down to Anderson and the uniform at the end of the sidewalk.

"You can remove the tape and go," I say to the uniform. "We're done here."

"Yes, sir," he says.

Anderson and I get in the car.

"Pull up a Jeremy Lubbock. We'll go pay him a visit."

"Got it," Anderson says, pulling up the name on his phone. "Found him. She was a piece of work."

"She was interesting," I agree, rubbing my fingertips over my mouth. "I didn't believe a word she said."

"I didn't either."

Jeremy lives about three miles away from Francesca. "I wonder what they do for a living that they're both home this time of day?"

"Looks like they work at the airport," Anderson says. "Makes sense. Shift work."

"That would explain it," I agree as I pull into the driveway behind a minivan. "Van. Could Jeremy be a family man?"

"There are toys in the yard," Anderson says with a sigh. "Well, shit."

"Shit indeed."

We get out of the car and walk to the front door. I ring the bell. A few seconds later, a woman in her early twenties with a baby on her hip opens the door.

"Yes?" she says, her smile faltering.

"I'm Detective Crawford, and this is my partner Officer Anderson."

"Oh God, is my dad okay?" she asks, tears filling her eyes.

"We are not here to inform anyone of a death or accident," I quickly assure her. "We're looking for Jeremy Lubbock."

"Oh." She blinks rapidly. "Of course. Come in."

We follow her inside.

"Jer!"

"I'm right here." A tall, lean man is standing at the top of the staircase, watching us. He descends. "How can I help you?"

"First, do you know a Francesca Smith?"

He frowns, and his eyes dart to his wife, then back to me.

"Yes. I work with her at the airport."

Good. Don't lie to me.

"She called in a burglary this morning and told us you've been harassing her at work. She's pretty sure you stole her mother's wedding band just to dick with her."

I watch them both carefully. How they react in the next second will tell me *everything*.

"You've got to be fucking kidding me," Jeremy's wife mutters, shaking her head. "I told you to call the cops two weeks ago."

Jeremy wipes his hand down his face. "Jesus."

"So, do you *have* the ring?" I ask.

"Fuck, no," he responds immediately. Now this guy, I believe. "I'm not the one who's been pursuing her. She's crazy, man."

"Batshit," his wife agrees. "Show him the texts."

"There are texts?" I ask.

"Oh, yeah. Here." Jeremy takes his phone out and proceeds to show me pages and pages of disturbing text messages. "This is where they start, about three weeks ago when I started the job. At first, it wasn't too crazy."

Can I call you?

Are you alone?

I think you're the nicest guy I've ever met.

"Why did she have your number?" Anderson asks.

"I don't know how she got it," Jeremy replies. "And I've changed it three times since she started texting. She always finds the new one. I can prove that I changed it."

"I believe you."

I do. There's no reason for him to lie to me about this, and as I flip through the texts, they get more and more disturbing.

I know you're there, you're just not answering me. Is it because of that stupid Karen? I know you don't really love her.

"Are you Karen?"

Jeremy's wife nods soberly. "Yeah. She started texting me, too. Telling me to stay away from *her man.*"

"Jesus," Anderson mutters, reading over my shoulder.

I want you to fuck me. I want you inside of me. I can make you so happy! I can make you come in ways you've never dreamed of.

"Creepy," I mutter, still flipping. Finally, I get to last night.

I can ruin you, you asshole. You think I can't? I can claim that you've stolen from me. I can tell the cops you raped me. That you've been after me for years, and no matter what I do, you won't leave me alone. I can RUIN YOUR FUCKING LIFE!! I'm not joking, Jeremy.

I raise a brow when I see the three dots winking at me at the bottom of the screen.

"Seems she has something to say right now."

We wait a few moments, all four of us staring at the small screen, and then the message comes through.

I told you I wouldn't stop fighting for you. I warned you.

"Looks like a whole bunch of threats to me," Anderson says.

"You can press charges for harassment," I inform Jeremy. "Between all of the proof on your phone and the bogus call to us this morning, you'll have no problems getting the charges to stick. I can go arrest her right now."

"Do it," Karen says, her voice full of urgency. "Right now, on behalf of both of us. She's been harassing me, too."

"Agreed," Jeremy says. "This is just nuts. And it's not just me anymore. My wife doesn't deserve this."

"Jeremy, before we go pick her up, I need you to be honest with me. Brutally honest, even with your wife standing right here. Have you *ever* had sex with Francesca Smith?"

"No." He looks me dead in the eye, his face hard with rage. "I've never touched her. I've barely spoken to her, and just at work. I love my wife."

"Okay, then." I nod and ask Jeremy to take screenshots of all of the texts and send them to me. "We'll go get her."

"Thank you," Karen says. "Thank you so much."

"WELL, THAT WAS a clusterfuck." Anderson presses a wet rag to his neck where Francesca bit him, making him bleed.

"One of the worst arrests I've been involved in, and I've seen plenty." I collapse behind my desk and sigh. "You need to go have that cleaned out properly and file a report."

"I'm most pissed about the extra paperwork this is going to generate," he says, shaking his head. I can't help but agree.

"I'm with you there. Go get stitched up and take the rest of the day off. In fact, I'm going to wrap up a few things and head out myself."

"Whoa. Detective Crawford of the SPD is taking time off?"

I flip him off, but he grins.

"You're a legend for working more hours than anyone else. What gives?"

I have a sexy redhead on my hands that I can't wait to see again.

But I don't say that. I'd rather not be the laughing stock of the department.

"Seeing your blood has me lightheaded," I lie, earning an eye roll.

"We've seen more blood than this."

"Are you going to go get stitched up before you pass out on my floor?"

"Yes, sir." He starts to walk away but stops himself and looks back at me. "Thank you. For teaching me."

"You've earned it. See you tomorrow. No calling in sick."

"No, sir."

I sigh and sit back in my chair. He's right, leaving early isn't my style. Before Starla, I'd hole up here for days on end, working through case after case.

But now that I have her, I can't get out of here fast enough.

She asked Luke and Nat the other night when a person starts to realize that it's time to slow down. When the priorities change.

I already feel that, and I'd be a fucking liar if I said it didn't scare me. Police work is all I know. It's been my first love for all of my adult life. That changing is terrifying to me.

But losing her is just as scary.

I pick up my phone and shoot her a text.

Leaving work early. Dinner?

I smile when her message comes through.

Chinese. I'm ordering. What do you want?

Her. I want her. But for tonight, I'll settle for Chinese.

Chicken chow mein. Extra eggrolls, unless you want to share yours.

I lock my office and walk through the bullpen to the parking garage.

Extra eggrolls it is.

seven

Starla

I'm getting damn sick and tired of waking up in a cold, empty bed.

Every night for the past week, Levi comes to my place. We have dinner, or we go out to eat. We walk along the waterfront. We make out a little—not nearly enough, if you ask me—and then he leaves.

I go to bed alone. I wake up alone.

It's freaking ridiculous.

I pad into the kitchen wearing a tank and yoga shorts, rubbing sleep from my eyes. My piano was delivered a few days ago, and I plan to sit at it all morning before I go to the studio with Jax and Meredith.

I've fallen into a routine here, which is new and foreign to me, but it's also soothing. I write in the morning, spend some time at the studio, and then I'm home in time to spend the evening with Levi. Over the weekend, I spent most of each day with Levi, exploring more of Seattle. He's become a constant in my life, in a very short period of time.

I don't know what I would do if he were suddenly gone.

And that thought scares me. Because just as I learned before, a person can be gone in the blink of an eye.

I frown, carrying my bottle of water to the piano. I set it on the floor, not wanting to chance leaving a water ring on the gleaming wood of the instrument, and noodle the keys, playing songs I've already written. Some have been recorded, some haven't yet.

When I'm warmed up, I reach for my notebook of music paper and a pencil and dig in, running lines over and over.

I know you want me to let you in

But hearts are messy

I frown. That doesn't sound good.

I know you want me to let you in

But this door on my heart is locked

Better. I write it down and then play the melody again. It's soft, a gentle ballad that will likely be played at weddings someday.

Before I know it, several hours have passed, and I think I have the song mostly worked out. The doorbell rings, pulling me out of my haze of creativity. I pad to the door and open it, surprised to see Joy and Lia smiling at me.

"We brought lunch," Joy announces, holding up a brown bag.

"And margaritas," Lia adds, making me grin. "We thought maybe you could use some friendly company."

Joy's head tilts to the side. "But if we're interrupting something—"

"No, come in." I move back so they can come inside, then shut the door behind them. "I'm sorry I'm still in my pajamas. I started writing as soon as I woke up and I haven't taken a break."

"Have you eaten?" Lia asks.

"Nope."

"Excellent," Joy says with a grin. "Because we have some delicious Mexican food in here, along with the margaritas."

"It's noon." I frown at the time.

"They're virgin ones," Lia says with a shrug. "Joy's preggers, so no drinking liquor in front of her. Also, it's Monday. And who couldn't use a margarita on a Monday?"

"I could," Joy says, raising her hand. "Virgin or otherwise, they're delish. What kind of song are you working on?"

"A ballad." I'm salivating at the sight of the chips and salsa Joy's currently setting on my table. Food is a great idea. "Do you want to hear it?"

"Yes," they answer in unison, both grinning.

"After you eat something," Joy adds, passing me a taco.

"Good call." I take the taco and devour it in about four bites. "I was hungrier than I thought."

"I brought tons of food," Lia assures me, passing me another taco. I pop a chip into my mouth and shimmy in my seat, happy to have them here.

"When is the baby due?" I ask Joy, eyeing her barely-round belly.

"This winter," she says while rubbing her hands over her midsection. "So far, the morning sickness is gone. Now, I just want to eat everything in sight. I'll gain a hundred pounds with this baby."

"No, you won't," Lia says, shaking her head. "You make good food choices. You can eat all the carrots you want."

"I don't want carrots. I want Doritos."

"Maybe eat more carrots than Doritos," I say with a laugh.

"How are things with Levi?" Joy asks, earning a glare from Lia that says *really*? "What? It's just a question."

"Things are good." I reach for another taco. "He's a great guy. Funny. Protective. Sexy as all get out."

"That's a Crawford thing," Joy says, nodding. "Sexy *and* smart."

"I just wish he'd use the sexiness a little more," I confess. "He says we're taking it slow, and it's *killing* me."

"That's sort of sweet, though," Lia says thoughtfully. "That he doesn't want to just jump into bed with you. Also, you should know, he's not dating you because of the stardom."

"We wouldn't be having this conversation if he was," I say with a sigh. "Because there have been plenty who have tried. None were successful. In fact, Levi's the first guy I've dated since Rick's accident."

Both women grow quiet, chewing thoughtfully. Maybe I shouldn't have said anything. I trust them, but I don't know them well. I don't want to make them uncomfortable.

Why did I even say that?

"I'm so sorry that happened to you," Lia says at last. "It must have been the most devastating thing."

"It was," I agree and nod. "But it was a long time ago, and it's time to live my life again. It's not like I've had to chase Levi."

"No, he's into you." Joy's voice is full of confidence. "I tried to antagonize him a bit last week, and he didn't fall for it. Because he's a cop, he doesn't like to say much about stuff, but he admitted that he likes you a lot. It was sweet."

"He's sweet," I murmur, looking down at the half-eaten taco in my hands. "He's the best."

"Okay, I'm ready for music," Lia says, shifting in her seat. "Whenever you're done eating."

"Awesome. I'd like to hear what you think of this one so far. It's a little different for me, but I think it's pretty."

I sit at the piano and begin the song I've been working on. There are a few rough spots that I have to mumble through because I don't have all of the lyrics ironed out. When I'm finished, I look up to find both women leaning on the piano, hanging on every note.

"Well?"

"Oh my God, so good," Joy says. "It's beautiful, Starla."

"We would be honest if it sucked," Lia adds. "But trust me. It doesn't."

"Thanks." I smile and make a tweak on the notepad. "I'm glad you guys came over. This was fun."

"Well, you're dating our brother-in-law," Lia says. "And we wanted to get to know you a little better."

"I'm glad," I repeat and then reach for my phone sitting on the top of the piano. Just as I grab it, it pings with an incoming message. "Sorry, I'm waiting for an email from my manager on something. I just need to check this real quick."

"No problem," Joy says. "We should probably head out anyway. I have to go feed that little kitten I rescued behind the clinic."

Joy's and Lia's voices fade as I read the email.

You fucking bitch. Did you think you could ignore my last email and I'd just go away? I won't be ignored! Who do you think you are? You're not special. There's a place in hell reserved for cunts like you. In fact, maybe I'll send you straight to hell, sooner than later.

I see you. I'm watching. Killing you, making you PAY for what you did, would be so damn easy. If you think I'm kidding, I've attached a photo of what I'd like to do to you.

There's a picture attached that makes me sick to my stomach. I drop the phone to the floor and grab a nearby wastebasket to hurl into, unable to run to the bathroom.

"Starla?"

"What's going on?"

"Honey, what is it?" Lia asks, wrapping her arm around my shoulders. "What was in that email?"

"Oh my God." I look up at Joy's voice and see her reading the email. "For fuck's sake."

"Let me see," Lia demands. Joy passes her the phone, and they switch places. Lia reads while Joy comforts me.

"It's just a maniac who likes scaring you," she says. But she's wrong.

"No," Lia says flatly, and the next thing I know, she's speaking into my phone, talking to Levi. "This is Lia. Joy and I are with Starla at her house, and we need you here, Levi. Starla's been threatened. Yep. We'll be here."

She hangs up, puts my phone to sleep, and sets it aside.

"He's on his way."

"I wish you hadn't called him," I whisper. I'm shaking. I'm dizzy. Blood rushes in my ears, through my head, making me unsteady.

"He's a cop, and he's your boyfriend," Joy reminds me, rubbing circles on my back. "He'll take care of this."

"Just a stupid fan. It happens sometimes."

"He didn't say he hated your new song," Lia says. "He fucking threatened to *kill you*."

I fold over the wastebasket again, heaving.

"Hey, he can't hurt you, honey," Joy says. "No one's going to hurt you."

"No. They're not."

My head comes up at the sound of Levi's voice. God, he looks good. I'm so relieved to see him, tears suddenly flow, and I can't stop them.

He folds me into his arms and holds me close, kissing my head and temple.

"You're okay," he says. "I promise, sweetheart, you're okay."

"Here." I open my phone and pass him the email. "Read it."

He's quiet, but I watch his eyes. They go from brown to black with pure rage as he reads the words and then sees the photo.

It's Meredith and me at Nordstrom a few weeks ago, shopping. But whoever it is used Photoshop to make it look like we're both dead. Bloody.

It's like something out of a horror movie.

"Fuck me," Levi growls. He taps on the screen, and then he pulls out his own phone and makes a call. "Yeah, it's Crawford. I just sent an email to you from Starla's email address. I need the original note traced. I'll wait while you open it."

Levi kisses me again and rubs his hand soothingly up and down my back.

"Yeah, I know. Great, work on it and keep me posted."

He ends the call and hugs me close again.

"Thanks for calling me," he says to Lia.

"Of course. We'll get out of your way. But, Starla, if you need *anything*, I'm just across the street. Don't hesitate to call."

"Thank you," I say with a watery smile. "And thank you for being here. For lunch and everything."

"Of course."

Both women hug me, and then they're gone, and it's just Levi and me, watching each other with sober eyes.

"It's probably nothing," I say at last, wiping the tears from my cheeks. "Just some asshole who wants to scare me. It happens."

I stand and pace the room, suddenly filled with nervous energy.

"How often does this happen, Star?"

I stop and look at him. "People send stupid messages and comment on my posts on Instagram all the time. *I hate your new song. You're not that pretty. I don't know what all the fuss is about, your talent is shit.*"

I shrug and pace into the kitchen where I pull a bottle of water out of the fridge and take a drink, the cold liquid soothing my hot throat.

"That's not the same thing, and you know it."

Nope. It's not the same thing. But I feel like if I dwell on what's in that email, I'll completely fall apart.

"Is it crazy that the part that fucked with me the most was seeing Meredith in that picture?" I scrub my hands over my face and walk out back to the pool area. I can sense the beginnings of fall in the air, and it feels good. Refreshing.

"No, it's not crazy," Levi says from behind me. I turn to find him leaning against the doorjamb, his hands in his pockets. He took his leather jacket off, and he's just in a white T-shirt. The sleeves are stretched tight around his muscular biceps.

"You don't have any tattoos," I say.

"No." He watches me carefully.

"I know, I'm all over the place. Maybe I just need to swim."

I strip out of my clothes and dive into the deep end. The water is cooler than normal this afternoon, but it's refreshing, as well.

I swim back and forth until my limbs are too tired to keep going. I climb out of the pool, and Levi is standing by with a big towel. He wraps it around me and pulls me to him, rocking us back and forth.

"We should talk about this."

"Did your person trace the email?" I ask, looking up into his face. He frowns, and I know the answer isn't what I want to hear.

"No. It's not traceable, unfortunately. But they're still going to work on it, see if there's a back door they're missing."

"I see." I lean against his chest and listen to his heartbeat for a moment. "I'm honestly a little surprised that this messed with me so much. I can let a *lot* roll off my shoulders. But Meredith . . ."

"Shh." He kisses my forehead. "Mer's fine. I've called Mark to let him know what's up, but she wasn't directly threatened in the email, sweetheart. I'd say you're the target, and it pisses me the fuck off."

His voice is hard again. I gaze up at him, so grateful that he's here.

"I don't want you to leave."

"I'm not going anywhere."

I nod and pull away, but his arms tighten, keeping me close.

I want him. I've never wanted anyone the way I want Levi Crawford, and trust me, that's fed my guilt in ways I don't want to think about right now.

I just know that I want him. Right now.

"Levi," I whisper, watching his Adam's apple bob as he swallows hard.

"Starla, you're upset." He doesn't pretend to not know what's going through my mind, and I appreciate that.

"Yes, I am. And I want *you*. I want you to make me forget, to make me *feel*. I feel alive with you, Levi."

He kisses my forehead, and his hands glide up and down my back, still covered with the towel.

"Sweetheart—"

"I'm not used to begging for sex, Levi, but if that's what you want, I will. Please."

He lifts me, cradling me in his arms as he stomps through my house and up the stairs to my bedroom. He sets me on my feet, and I let the towel spill to the floor.

"Jesus, you're beautiful."

"And you're overdressed." I pull his shirt out of the waistband of his blue jeans and up over his head, then toss it on the tile. Before I unfasten his pants, I let my fingertips roam over his warm, smooth skin, taking in every defined muscle.

"You're hot."

He grins. "Thanks. I'm glad you approve." He swallows again. "And if you keep touching me like that, this won't last long."

I laugh, delighted with him, and reach for his pants. But before I can continue stripping him, he waves my hands aside and hurries out of his jeans, kicks them aside, and leads me back onto the bed.

"I've dreamed of this for weeks," he confesses as his fingertips glide up and down my torso, from my neck to my belly button and back again. "You need to know that once this happens, there's no going back, Starla. This isn't a one-night stand for me."

"Message received." I brush my fingers through his salt-and-pepper hair, loving the way the strands feel in my hand. "You make me feel things no one else ever has, and that both scares and thrills me."

His brown eyes find mine, and while holding my gaze, he tugs my nipple into his mouth, gently plucking it between his teeth.

"Just enjoy," he whispers and begins to explore me as if this were our first time together. As if he can't get enough of looking at me, touching me.

I sigh and close my eyes, circling my hips in invitation.

"Watch me," he commands.

Two simple words, but when they come from Levi, they send shivers down my spine. I can't take my eyes off him as he kisses down my sternum, licks my navel, then nudges his shoulders between my legs and grins as he stares down at the most intimate part of me.

"Beautiful," he mutters before licking me from pussy to clit, sending shock waves through my body, making me arch off the bed.

"Holy shit!"

"Easy," he croons as he plants one hand flat against my lower stomach, holding me in place as he feasts on me, taking and giving so much back at the same time.

I can't keep my eyes open. I can't keep from *moving*. I shake my head back and forth and circle my hips as the pressure builds at the base of my spine.

"Levi, I'm going to—"

"Do it."

I can't hold back any longer. I come apart at the seams,

crying out in delight as wave after wave of pleasure rolls over my body.

Before I can catch my breath, Levi covers me, cradling my head in his hands as he slips inside of me and holds steady, watching my face with rapt attention.

"Condom?" I ask breathlessly.

"Already took care of it while you were delirious." His grin is wicked as he pulls back and then sinks back in, setting a steady pace that makes me grasp onto his ass for dear life. "God, Starla."

"So good," I agree, and feel him tense with the effort to keep his own orgasm at bay. "Give in."

"Too fast."

I cradle his face in my hands. "Give in," I repeat and watch as he does just that, letting his orgasm take over.

It's the sexiest thing I've ever seen in my life.

eight

Levi

"You're going to be the death of me."

I'm playing with her hair as she lies on my chest, both of us struggling to catch our breath.

"That's not funny." She frowns up at me and then turns away, climbing out of the bed and padding into the en suite. I hurry into the other bathroom on this floor, clean up, and when I return to the bedroom, Starla is pulling on her clothes.

"It's just an expression," I remind her, uneasy with the stiff lines of her shoulders and back. "You know that, right?"

"Right." She sighs and turns to look at me. "But after Rick, jokes about dying just aren't funny, Levi."

"Who's Rick?"

She stares at me for a long moment. "Do you live under a rock?"

"Keeping up with pop culture really isn't my strong suit." I tug on my jeans but don't bother fastening them or pulling on my shirt. "So, who's Rick?"

"He was my fiancé," she says as calmly as if she were telling me the temperature outside. "And he died."

"Start from the beginning."

"Let's go downstairs," she suggests, already walking ahead of me out of the room and down the stairs. "Rick was a race car driver. I met him at an event, and we were inseparable after that day."

Being jealous of a dead man isn't something I'm proud of, but here we are.

"He was successful and loved the thrill of racing. It scared the hell out of me. I wouldn't get in one of those death traps if my life depended on it. And Rick always assured me he was safe. Careful. I believed him."

She fills a kettle full of water and sets it on the stove to boil. I sit in a stool at the island, watching her move about the kitchen, pulling out cheese, crackers, and fruit.

"He asked me to marry him before my Belladonna tour, and things were good. We were on the same page about life goals."

"And what were those?" I ask, pulling her out of her reverie.

She blinks at me twice and then answers. "No kids, focus on career, retire early."

"Okay, and then?" I don't ask her if those are still her goals. We'll get to that later.

"I was on tour, and he was with me in Dallas for a show. He had a race the next day, and I told him not to come to the show in Dallas, that he should be in Florida where the race was, getting rest and practice. But Rick had a thing about missing any of my shows. He thought it was bad luck."

She rolls her eyes and shakes her head as she places the snacks on a cutting board.

"He flew out to Florida after the show, but it was a late-night flight, and by the time he got there, got settled at the hotel, and headed to the race track, he hadn't had much rest to speak of. I was so damn irritated with him."

The last sentence is a whisper as she pushes the board to the middle of the island. When the whistle blows on the water, she pulls the kettle off the flame and reaches for two mugs and some teabags.

"Tea?" she asks.

"Sure."

I don't give a fuck about tea, or cheese and crackers for that matter, but I'm not about to stop her. She's on a roll.

"So, he called me, and he was kind of whiny about how tired he was. I was frustrated with him because I'd told him to *go* the day before. In fact, I think my exact words were, *get the fuck to Florida. You've seen the show.*

"I think that hurt his feelings, or he was just stubborn and more determined to stay after that."

She shrugs a shoulder and pops a piece of Swiss into her mouth, chewing thoughtfully.

"Either way, I didn't coddle him during that call. I told him he was tired because he was a stubborn ass, and I didn't feel sorry for him. I told him to suck it up and deal with it, and good luck."

She stares at the cracker in her hands, then looks up at me.

"I didn't say *I love you*. I didn't say anything nice during that call, actually."

I remember the crash now, but I wait patiently and let her finish telling me herself.

"The next thing I know, I'm getting a call from Bobby, Rick's manager, who was with him, telling me that Rick screwed up in the race and was in a massive accident." She looks me square in the eyes, and the turmoil churning within her is almost my undoing. "The car exploded, and he didn't survive. I saw the crash on TV before they cut to commercial. I was praying that he somehow made it out alive, but he didn't."

"I'm so sorry, sweetheart."

"Yeah." She sets the cracker aside and dunks her teabag in the hot water. "It was pretty horrible. And I had a bad case of survivor's guilt because I was so mean to him that morning. And for a million other reasons."

"You didn't know."

"No, but I feel guilty all the same. I told him to suck it up and just deal, and it probably cost him his life."

"That's not true."

"It's absolutely true. He could have pulled out of the race altogether and cited medical problems. But I had to challenge him, and he died because of it."

"He died because he didn't listen to common sense and get rest when he should have," I counter. "He was an adult."

"I suppose." But she doesn't sound convinced.

"What else are you feeling guilty about?"

"Everything," she says without even thinking it over. "It's why I work so damn hard. If I'm working, sinking all of my energy into the job, I don't have time to think about Rick and that whole clusterfuck. But it caught up to my health, and my doctor *made* me take this three-month vacation."

"How is it affecting your health?"

"I was getting dizzy. I passed out twice on the road. I was convinced I had a brain tumor, but the doctor said it was exhaustion and ordered mandatory rest."

"Good."

She raises her brow and takes a sip of her tea. "I hadn't slept with anyone after Rick until you. That's why I didn't text or call you after. Because I felt a *massive* amount of guilt for not only being with you but also enjoying it so much."

"Starla, Rick would want you to move on with your life. He would want you to be happy."

She shakes her head adamantly. *No.*

"Of course, he would," I continue. "He loved you."

"No. He wouldn't." She takes a deep breath. "I can't believe I'm about to tell you this. I probably should have made you sign an NDA when we started seeing each other."

"That's the second and last time you'll insult either of us like that."

Her cheeks darken with shame. "I'm sorry. You're right."

"Tell me."

"About a month or so before he died, Rick was filling out new insurance paperwork, life insurance and that sort of thing. Doing what he did for a living is dangerous, and he always had an updated will. He was making sure I was the beneficiary on everything since we were just a few months from being married. Anyway, I can't remember exactly what led to it, but I said something about wearing black for a whole year if he died, out of respect. I said it in a joking way, you know?"

I nod, waiting for her to tell me more.

"And *he* said, '*No, you'll get in that coffin with me, babe. If I die, you die. There's no happily ever after without me.*'"

I've never wanted to punch the hell out of a dead man so badly in my life.

"I laughed at him, sure that he was continuing the joke, but he was dead serious. He was like, '*no, you're mine, and if one of us dies, the other does, too.*' I blew him off, and we never talked about it again."

"Starla, that's not a normal thing for someone to say to a person they supposedly love."

"Well, I didn't grow up in a typical loving family, and I'm not using that as an excuse, but I just blew him off because he was only thirty-two. I never expected him to actually *die*."

"Of course, you didn't."

"I was so fucked up after it happened." She closes her eyes and shakes her head mournfully. "And I will admit—to you—that I thought about killing myself."

My hands fist on the countertop, the movement catching her eye.

"Are you okay?"

"No. Keep going."

She pauses. "I had it all planned out. I had a bottle full of a mish-mash of pills that I'd been prescribed for anxiety and insomnia. A bunch of stuff. And I was just going to take them all at once and go to sleep."

My gut churns. My eyes burn. The thought of Starla hurting herself, of never knowing her is a searing slash to my very soul.

"What stopped you?"

"Meredith called me that afternoon and said she was on her way to spend a few days with me. That Mark had things handled at home, and she wanted to be with me. It gave me something to be happy about. Something to look forward to. And I knew that if I followed through with my plan, she and Jax would be devastated, and I didn't want to put them through that.

"So, I took the bottle into the bathroom and flushed all

of the pills. Since then, I still don't sleep well, but I refuse to take meds for it. I never fill the prescriptions. It's not because I want to hurt myself, but because I don't *want* them. I have been doing fine."

I shift my head to the side as if what she said didn't make sense at all.

Because it doesn't.

"Everything you just said does not sound *fine.*"

"I know, but I really am. After the first six months or so, I fell into a rhythm. Record, promote, tour. Over and over again. Constant work. Come to Seattle to see Jax and Mer and the kids, then back to it. I worked hard, and I'm proud of what I've accomplished in the past five years. My career has skyrocketed, thanks to that hard work."

"And you're dizzy and passing out."

She narrows her eyes at me. "I went to the doctor and took his advice to rest. I hated the idea of it, trust me, but here I am. And it worked out because I reconnected with you, and I get to see Mer and Jax whenever I want. I'm writing songs, and I'm dancing, but I'm not fixated on the work anymore.

"And, yes, I feel guilty that I enjoy you so much. That not just the sex but *everything* feels amazingly easy with you. Rick would *not* want that. But, damn it, I'm here, and I'm not going to just *exist* anymore. I'm going to live my life."

"Good girl," I whisper, watching her from the other side of the island. I want to hurry to her and sweep her into my arms, kiss her silly.

"You can run away if you want to. I wouldn't blame you. I'm a mess."

I stand, but I don't run away. I walk around to her and pull her against me, smiling against her hair when she clings to me in relief.

"I'm not going anywhere."

"Okay. Good." She kisses my bare chest. "You should have put a shirt on because telling you that story when you're half-naked was really distracting."

"You did great."

MY PHONE RINGS beside the bed in the early morning light, and I answer before the first ring is finished.

"Crawford," I whisper as I pad to the bathroom, closing the door behind me.

"Hey, it's Matt Montgomery. Sorry to call so early, but I'm at the Lubbock residence. Jeremy and Karen. You were here a couple of days ago?"

"Yeah, he's being stalked by Francesca Smith."

"You might want to get over here," Matt says grimly. "Now."

"On my way."

I don't question him further. I end the call and splash cold water on my face and over my hair. I quickly brush my teeth, push my fingers through my hair, and walk into the bedroom to pull on some clothes.

"What is it?" Starla asks from the bed, her voice heavy with sleep. She actually slept the entire night.

"I need to go follow up on a case I had a few days ago. There's an emergency, it seems. I'll be back as soon as I can."

"I'm fine," she insists and rubs her eyes. "Honestly, I am. Go do your job. I'm safe here."

I prop my hands on my hips and watch her. The threat yesterday was real, and not something to take lightly.

"I'll assign a uniform to sit on the street in an unmarked car."

"There's no need for that."

"Humor me." I kiss her lips and hurry out. "I'll call when I can."

"Bye!"

It's before six, so the drive through the city to the other side of town doesn't take long. The Lubbock house has been taped off, and the street is blocked off with cruisers.

"Crawford," I say immediately to the uniform at the door.

"Yes, sir. Montgomery is inside." He passes me a pair of sterile booties to go over my shoes.

I nod and step in, then stop in my tracks.

There is blood *everywhere*. On the walls, the floor, up the stairs to the second floor.

Red and fresh.

"Jesus," I mutter, pulling latex gloves out of my pocket and immediately pulling them on, then slip the booties over my shoes. This crime scene is intense and won't be tainted with any of my prints or DNA.

I'm too fucking smart for that.

"Up here," Montgomery calls out, and I do my best to avoid most of the blood on the stairs as I climb them. "In the bedroom."

I stop at the doorway. "What do we have?"

Matt squats beside the body of Francesca. "This is one of two vics."

"Where's the other?"

His eyes turn up to mine. "In the bathroom. Before you go

in there, know that it's maybe the most gruesome thing I've ever seen in my twenty years on the force."

I cock a brow. "I take it that's where all the blood came from? Because she's not stabbed." I indicate Francesca's prone form.

"Affirmative," Matt says with a nod. "Francesca was shot. Once."

And from the looks of it, in the head.

I walk into the bathroom and have to close my eyes against the immediate onslaught of nausea. I've seen *everything* on this job.

Or I thought I had, until this.

"Fuck me," I mutter and feel Montgomery walk up behind me, taking in the scene with me.

"Yeah."

Karen Lubbock, or what's left of her, is in the bathtub. She's cut from her throat to her pubic bone, and all of her internal organs are no longer internal. More blood practically paints the walls and pools on the floor. Her head is scalped. Her eyes are gouged out.

I glance into the sink and have to cover my mouth. "Are those her teeth?"

"Looks like it."

"Fuck, Matt, she literally dismantled her."

"We think Karen answered the door to Fran, and Fran immediately stabbed her, pushing her inside. Kept stabbing her, and dragged her up the stairs, through the bedroom, and in here. Karen was long dead when she was disemboweled."

"She was more than disemboweled," I reply. "I don't even know what this is."

"Jeremy Lubbock was at work, working an extra night shift.

Whether Fran knew that or not, we don't know."

"She probably did." I bend over and look in the tub, then immediately regret my decision. "Was she pregnant?"

"Yeah."

"Jesus Christ, Matt."

"Jeremy came in and found them. He retrieved his handgun and shot Fran. Once. Then called us."

"Where is he? And the kids?"

"His parents came to get the kids, and he's at the police station, giving a statement and being evaluated."

I walk out of the bathroom, unable to look any longer at the holes in Karen's head where her eyes should be.

Fran is on the floor, staring up at the ceiling. Lifeless.

"I arrested her two days ago for stalking and harassment. She bit the hell out of Anderson, sending *him* to the hospital."

"I know," Matt says. "She posted bail yesterday morning."

"And came here seeking revenge."

"Looks that way."

"She was one fucked-up woman. You're not going to charge him." It's not a question, and Matt shakes his head no.

"It was self-defense."

"Agreed. God. How can I help?"

"I'll need copies of your reports, and Jeremy asked to speak to you. So, if you don't mind going to the office and talking with him, I'd appreciate it."

"Done. What do you say to someone whose pregnant wife was literally gutted in his bathroom?"

Matt just shakes his head. "I'm so fucking pissed off, I would kill her myself if he hadn't finished the job. And that makes me a shitty cop."

"It makes you a good cop and a good man. You have a wife."

"And a baby on the way," he says. "I can't imagine it."

"The medical examiner on the way?"

"He's outside. I asked him to wait until after you got here. I'd also like you to take a look around, make sure nothing is different from two days ago when you were here. I don't want to miss anything."

"I'll look around on my way out, but aside from the blood, nothing stands out."

He nods, and I walk out, checking through the rooms I was in before. It doesn't look like Fran was in there. Nothing is broken or moved. Nothing seems suspicious.

But when I turn to walk outside, one word is written in red on the back of the door.

Mine.

nine

Starla

I've gone over this line sixty times, and I just can't get it right. I don't love the melody, and I certainly don't like the lyrics.

I lean my forehead on the piano. I've been at it too long. I'm tired, which is unusual for me at midnight, but I can't go to bed.

I haven't heard from Levi all day. I knew he was busy at work, so I didn't try to text or call until after six, but he never responded.

And that's not like him.

I didn't want to seem like the crazy girlfriend, so I didn't try again, but I'm worried now. And maybe a *little* crazy.

So, I try to call again, but it goes to voicemail.

I know he keeps the ringer on for work, so either something's wrong, or he's ghosting me. Both options give me anxiety.

I decide to throw caution to the wind and call Lia.

"Hello?"

"Hey, it's Starla. I know it's super late, so I'm sorry if I woke you."

"You didn't," she assures me. "What's up? Are you okay?"

"I'm fine, but I haven't heard back from Levi all day, and I'm kind of worried. Have you guys talked to him?"

"I haven't, but let me ask Wyatt." She doesn't cover the phone when she turns her attention to her husband, who must be sitting close by. "Have you talked to Levi tonight? . . . When? . . . Is he okay?"

"What did he say?"

"He said he talked to him earlier this evening. Levi was at home."

I stand and march to my handbag, grabbing it and my keys. "What's his address?"

She rattles it off. "Oh, you can park under his building in one of the guest slots."

"Perfect, thanks."

"No problem."

She hangs up, and I hurry to my car, pull out of the driveway, and head toward town, following the instructions on the GPS on my phone.

I notice that the cop who's been parked outside my place all day follows me, but I don't care.

The least Levi could have done was text me back to tell me that he was okay and just needed some time alone. Hell, I understand needing some space. *Needs space* is my middle name.

But ignoring me? That's not okay. And, yes, I see the irony here. If this is half as bad as he felt when I didn't reply to him after our first night together, I feel even worse about it now. That was a bitchy thing to do, and I'll regret it forever.

I find his address, and just like Lia said, I pull under the building and find an empty space marked *guest*. I hurry to the elevator and punch in his floor.

When the doors open, I hurry out and down the hallway to his door, pounding on it when I get there.

It takes about thirty seconds for him to answer. Maybe he was asleep? I don't know, but when he pulls open the door, I scowl at what I see before me.

Levi's hair is disheveled, his face is dark with stubble, and he's only wearing boxers.

"If I interrupted you with someone—"

"For fuck's sake," he mutters, taking my hand and pulling me inside. "No one is here, Star."

"Were you sleeping?"

"Unfortunately, no." He sinks into a reclining chair and rubs his hand over his eyes. There's a bottle of scotch next to him, along with a half-full glass.

"Are you drunk?"

"No." His brown eyes hold mine as I perch on the edge of the couch across from him.

"You look horrible."

I want to climb into his lap and hold him tightly, to assure him that whatever is going on will be okay.

"Thanks."

"Levi, what's going on? Why didn't you reply to my calls or texts?"

"I'm sorry about that," he says, rubbing his eyes again as if he's trying to scrub something away. "I should have replied. It's just been a rough day."

"I see that." My voice is soft as I watch him. "Did someone die?"

He grins humorlessly and looks over at me. "Yeah. Two someones, actually. Well, three if you count the baby."

"What in the world? I didn't think you worked homicide?"

"And I won't be." He takes a sip of his scotch. "Not after today. I'm not going to fill your head with what I saw today, sweetheart. And I'm not great company right now, so I just came home to brood and get a little drunk."

"I guess being with a cop means there will be tough days like this."

His eyes meet mine again in surprise. "There are some rough days, yes."

"So, in the future, if there are bad moments, can I expect you to just disappear? I shouldn't worry? I'm not trying to flip you shit for this, Levi. I'm honestly not, I just want to be ready if it happens again."

"Come here."

Finally. I comply, and he pulls me into his lap and buries his face in my neck, holding on tightly.

"You can always talk to me," I remind him as I push my fingers through his hair, soothing us both. "Always. I might not understand, but that doesn't mean I can't listen."

"Today was too horrible," he mumbles against my skin. "Too gruesome to talk about. And I *can't* really talk about it. But you're right, I should have gone to you rather than try to protect you from it because having you here for less than ten minutes has already calmed me."

I smile and kiss his temple. "I'm glad. Are you tired?"

"Bone-tired."

"Does this thing recline?"

He reaches to the side, and suddenly, we're rocked back.

I stretch out, half on him and half off, my head on his chest. We don't say anything at all, we just listen to the stillness of the night around us in the apartment. Before long, Levi is snoring softly.

With my ear pressed to his chest, listening to the soothing, rhythmic beat of his heart, I follow him into a deep slumber.

"FOR CHRIST'S SAKE, Jax, you're going to break my freaking tailbone."

I rub the spot with indignation, pissed as all get out that Jax just threw me on my ass.

"Stick the landing, and you won't have a sore ass," he retorts. "You've done that move a million times."

"Yeah, when I was in shape for the tour, not when I've been off the road for a month." I stand and walk to the edge of the studio to retrieve my water bottle. "Why are you so damn intense today?"

"I'm just doing my job."

"No." I cock my head to the side, watching him. "You don't usually toss me around like that unless you're pissed. What are you pissed about?"

He turns his back on me and yanks his white towel off the bar to wipe his face.

"Logan irritates the fuck out of me sometimes."

"Lover's spat." I nod and take another drink. "That'll do it. For the betterment of my ass, could you tone it down just a smidge? I'm going to be bruised."

"He can be so damn inconsiderate."

I suppose we'd better hammer this out so I don't leave here with a broken wrist. "What did he do? You guys don't usually fight."

"His mother," Jax says with a sigh, making me grin. "It's not funny. That woman is *the worst*."

"What did she do?"

"She wants us to come to dinner tomorrow night."

"How horrifying of her." I smile as he glares at me.

"We already had plans, Star. Tickets to see a show we've wanted to see for a long time, and they weren't cheap. I've been looking forward to it for weeks."

"Gotcha. Okay, so Logan just tells her it'll have to be another night."

"One would think. But, no. No, he pretty much does whatever his mom wants him to do. So, instead of seeing the show, we're going to have dinner with *that woman*."

"Why can't he just tell her you have other plans?"

"Because she has cancer," Jax says and holds up a hand. "Now before you call me insensitive, hear me out. She has stage 0 breast cancer. The tiny lump has been removed, and the doctors don't even suggest she have a mastectomy or any other treatment. It's just gone. But she calls the goddamn *c*-card as often as she can, and *he falls for it*."

"Yikes." I scrunch up my face in sympathy. "Yeah, it does sound like she's using it as a way to manipulate Logan."

"Yes!" Jax points to me. "Exactly! But when I said that, you'd have thought I told him to just put her to sleep to put her out of her misery. He was *livid*."

"Maybe the cancer scared him, even if it was minor." I shrug. "I don't know, I'm not good at family stuff. When did it happen?"

"Two weeks ago."

"Give it a little time. He'll be better."

"In the meantime, I have to have dinner with her, watch her *wipe his mouth* with her napkin, and smile the whole time."

"We do ridiculous things for love."

Jax laughs and cues up the next song. "Okay, now that I've got that off my chest, shall we try this again?"

"I don't know, are you going to maim me?"

"No, drama queen."

"Takes one to know one."

The music starts as Jax laughs and reaches for my hand, easily guiding me around the floor in the familiar routine we've been working on. It's a slight change from the one we already had for this song; I just like to mix things up once in a while.

This will be a nice change when it's time to go out on the road again.

We run through it twice more, and each time, I stick the landing perfectly. No more falling on my ass.

"Okay, I was throwing too hard," Jax says. "I'm sorry."

"I'm gonna live." I plant a kiss on his cheek as Levi walks through the door and narrows his eyes on Jax.

"Do I have to kill you, man?" Levi asks.

"Nah." Jax holds out his hand to shake Levi's. "She just can't keep her hands off me."

"This room is suddenly full of male ego." I roll my eyes. All of a sudden, one of my most famous ballads comes through the speakers, and to my utter shock, Levi sweeps me into his arms and leads me into an easy slow dance across the floor. "Well, look at you, fancy-pants."

I wouldn't expect a man as big as Levi to move so effortlessly. It's sexy as hell to be in his strong arms, moving around the room.

He's singing along with the music, too, his voice a smooth baritone.

"I don't know if I've ever been so turned on by someone singing my own song to me," I confess with a soft voice.

"You write good music," is all he says before he begins singing again, leading me in the sexiest slow dance in the history of the world.

"Thanks for coming to get me."

"I was glad when you asked," he admits.

Jax came and got me and brought me to the studio, and I asked Levi to pick me up since we had plans to go out for dinner anyway.

"Have you had any other contact from the psycho?" he asks.

"No, thank goodness. Everything has been blissfully drama-free. Have you had dancing lessons?" I ask.

"Not unless you count watching *Dancing with the Stars*." He smiles down at me, pure joy radiating from him, and I'm completely intoxicated. This is a new side to Levi, one I've never seen before.

He tugs me closer and grinds against me, making me laugh.

"Hey, none of that," Jax calls from the edge of the room. "Get a room, Crawford."

"That's the plan," Levi mutters as he leans in to kiss my cheek. "Let's get out of here, sweetheart."

"I thought you'd never ask."

"I CAN HONESTLY say I've never had sex in a police car before."

We're sitting in the restaurant in a circular booth, next to each other. Levi's hand is on my still-tingling thigh.

"That makes two of us," he says with a smile and leans in to whisper in my ear. "But it won't be the last time."

We're not young adults. Keeping our hands to ourselves shouldn't be difficult. And yet, as soon as we made it from the studio to his car, I was straddling his lap, and his hand was down my yoga pants. It was fast and dirty, and so damn satisfying.

"Focus on the menu," Levi says beside me, not looking my way.

"I am." It's totally a lie.

"Squeezing your legs together like that gives you away."

I glance up at him and then break out into a laugh. "Who knew I had *this* side to me?"

"It seems we're bringing out new sides of each other."

"Hi, I'm Candy."

I look up to find a bored waitress in her early twenties holding a notepad and a pen. "What can I get you?"

She hasn't even looked at us, which is fine with me because I'm not disguised today.

"I'll have the salmon Caesar salad," I begin. "With an extra side of bread. Carbs are my soul mate."

She smirks, but she still doesn't look our way. "And for you, sir?"

"New York strip, medium rare, with the wild rice and a side green salad. I'd also like some bread."

"Okay," she says, jotting it all down. She glances up when she reaches for the menus and then stops cold when she sees me. "Oh, God. You're Starla."

"No, I—"

"Holy *shit*! I'm your biggest fan, like . . . ever. I know all the songs. And when you had that cameo in the movie with Adam Levine? Holy shit, *so good.*"

"Uh, thanks."

"Can we get some photos? And your autograph?"

"Later," Levi interrupts, glaring at Candy. "After we've had a chance to enjoy our meal, please."

"Oh. Right." She nods but then frowns. "Wait. Are you one of those stars who gets pissed when people just want to talk about how much your work means to them? Because I have to be honest, I think that's bullshit. As your fan, I've bought *everything* you've ever recorded, and concert tickets, too. Like, you're rich because of me."

"Right," I reply, completely pissed off and ready to just *go.* At this point, she'll probably spit in our food anyway. I've learned from experience, there is no bouncing back from this. She's already pissed off, and neither Levi nor I have done anything wrong. "It's awesome that you're such a big fan. I really appreciate it. Levi, we can just go."

"Oh, now you don't want to eat here?" Candy demands, propping her hands on her hips. "If you don't want to be recognized, you shouldn't leave your damn house."

"Wow," Levi says, crossing his arms over his chest. "Why do you think you can speak to her like that?"

"Well, because I'm her *biggest* fan," she says, and I can feel my cheeks blazing with embarrassment and anger. "Also, you should reply to your email."

I stop cold. No way. There's no way we just happened to

come in and eat where my stalker works. What are the odds of that?

Zero.

I'm being ridiculous. She probably just sent some fan mail that I didn't see. I shouldn't automatically jump to the worst-possible conclusion.

I want out of here.

"I'd like to go," I say to Levi as I glance around the restaurant. Other customers have stopped eating and are watching us with rapt interest. Some have even taken out their phones to record the incident. "Please, they're recording us."

"No problem," Levi says, scooting out of the booth and reaching for my hand.

"You had drinks," Candy says. "You can't just leave without paying for them."

"Yes, they can." A man walks up behind Candy, surprising her. "I'm *so* sorry for the harassment from my employee. This is not how we run our business. You're fired."

"What?" Candy demands.

"Get out," he says and turns to us. "I understand that you want to go, but come back anytime for a meal on us."

"Thanks," Levi says with a nod and pulls me close to his side as he leads me out of the restaurant. I tuck my face into his shoulder, trying to avoid being recorded by the phones pointed at us.

"That was a disaster," I say as we sit in his car. "I'm *so* sorry."

"What are you sorry for? That girl was *ridiculous*."

"Oh, that was tame compared to some I've met." My heart is racing and in my throat. "At least she didn't touch me."

"Christ," he mutters, putting the car in gear and driving

away from the restaurant. "Why are people so ridiculous? Why couldn't she have just quietly told you she enjoyed your work? Then we could have gotten on with our day."

"Most do that," I concede. "Ninety-nine percent of the time, people are gracious and kind, and just want to say hello. The other one percent is a little . . . odd."

"That's a polite way of putting it."

"Well, it's true. That whole scene will be all over social media and the tabloids within the hour—if it isn't already. I'm sorry for that because *your* face is there, too. And now people will dig into who you are, and it could be uncomfortable for you."

"I'm a big boy," Levi says with a sigh. "I'm fine. I don't give two shits about social media. I just don't want anyone to ever speak to you like that."

"Thank you."

"Are you still hungry?"

"Hell yes, I am."

He grins over at me. "Should we go get some Red Mill and take it back to my place?"

"That's perfect. I didn't really want to be good with a salad anyway. A burger sounds delicious."

"Done. But we're getting an extra order of fries because last time you ate half of mine."

"Why are you so protective of your fries?"

"Because I'm *hungry*."

"We'd better get two extra orders."

"You're really hungry."

"Sex in a cop car does that to me."

ten

Starla

"Fuck me," I mumble as I page through my Instagram. I'm in Levi's bed, the sheet wrapped around my naked body. I can hear Levi in the shower, blissfully unaware of the social media shitstorm that I'm watching.

There are videos of the whole scene—from different angles, of course. The comments below them range from *whoa, what a bitch! The waitress just wanted a photo!* to *why don't people leave celebrities alone when they're trying to live a normal life?*

There are more still photos, some zooming in on Levi.

"What in the hell?" I read the caption on one of the pictures.

Does anyone know who the tall drink of water is? I don't recognize him. Is he famous?

And the comments . . .

He's not famous. I did a Google image search, and it looks like he's a cop in Seattle.

Love his salt and pepper hair!

What does Starla want to do with an old dude? She's way too good for that. Hell, I'd fuck her.

In your dreams, asshole.

Maybe he's her bodyguard?

Oh, that could be.

"What are you scowling at?" Levi asks as he walks into the bedroom, naked as the day he was born. My eyes feast on him, taking in lean muscle and smooth, tan skin. He's hot as hell, and anyone who thinks differently can bite me.

"This turned into a social media mess," I reply. "I'm surprised the publicity team hasn't started texting me yet."

"It can't be that big of a deal," he says as he slips on a clean pair of boxer briefs. "That chick was out of line."

"Photos and videos spin things," I mutter. "And it pisses me off that they've dragged you into this."

I whip the covers off and reach for my clothes, yanking them on in jerking motions.

I'm so damn *pissed*.

And who the hell am I to think that I can have any kind of normal relationship, with Levi or anyone else? This will *always* happen. The media and *fans* will twist it to be something ugly.

"Starla."

"I think maybe I should go home. I'll call an Uber."

"Hold on."

"No, it's better this way." I shake my head as I slip my feet into my shoes. "It's just not going to work out between us, Levi, and I was silly to think that it might. It's not fair to do this to either of us. To open us up to gossip and scrutiny. You didn't ask for this."

"Stop moving."

His voice is hard, catching my attention, and my gaze swings to his. He's pissed off. His jaw is clenched, his hands balled into fists.

"What the fuck, Starla? I'm not a child. I'm capable of making my own life choices, and if being in a relationship with a ridiculously famous woman is one of those choices, well, it's mine to make."

"I just think—"

"I said stop," he snaps, and I blink at him in surprise. "Maybe you're right. Maybe I shouldn't want to be with you, but it has nothing to do with what *strangers* are saying about us on platforms I don't give a rat's ass about, and everything to do with the fact that you suddenly seem to think I'm a child that needs protecting. I'm *not* a child."

"I know you're not."

"The other night, after one of the worst days I've had on the force, you sought me out and comforted me. You said there would be rough days, and you're right. Well, same goes, sweetheart. That's just life."

He walks to me. Slowly. Deliberately.

"Now, we're going to get you back out of all these clothes. But the first thing you need to take off is your insecurities. If we're in this together, we're *in it*. Together. Whether I've had a rough day at work, or you have. Or anything else that comes up."

I stare up at him in wonder as he peels my clothes off, and when I'm standing naked before him—both physically and emotionally—he picks me up and takes me to the bed, laying me down gently on the soft linens.

"You're amazing," he whispers, kissing over my shoulders and up my neck to my lips. "Stunning. Smart. Kind."

"I'm not always kind."

"Liar." He bites my lip, then kisses my chin and works his way down to one breast. "You're kind and sweet. And when it's just you and me, it doesn't matter if ten million people know your face or want to know about your life."

"I have twenty-five million followers," I say, sassing him.

He cocks a brow. "None of them are here. It's just you and me."

His hand blazes a trail down my belly to my core.

"You don't belong to them." He slips two fingers inside me, sending my hips up off the bed. "You belong to *me.*"

My eyes find his as his fingers work me over, and his lips latch around a nipple.

"Who gives a shit what anyone else thinks?" he says when he lets go of my flesh with a loud pop.

"I don't like them saying horrible things about you."

I gasp as he presses the pad of his thumb against my clit.

"They can't hurt me." He watches me with hot brown eyes as I climb higher and higher, riding the delicious wave of an impending orgasm.

But before I get there, Levi reaches for a condom, slides it on, and sinks inside me until he's buried balls-deep. And then he stops. We're both gasping for breath, staring at each other intently.

"*They* can't hurt me. You're mine, Starla. You've been mine for a long time. Maybe forever. It just took me more than forty years to find you."

Tears spring to my eyes. My God, where did this amazing man come from?

"So all we have to worry about is what's happening right

here, between us. Fuck the rest of them."

I press on his shoulder, and he rolls, switching our position. I'm riding him now and grinding down on him with every stroke, sending electricity through every nerve ending of my body. Being with Levi is *so different* from being with anyone else.

Anyone.

It's like this is where I was supposed to be all along.

"Same," I whisper as I lean down and press my lips to his. "We belong to each other. And you're right, I'm too damn old to give a shit about what everyone else thinks about my love life. I'm happy. And if you're happy too, that's all that matters."

He grins and wraps his arms around me, holding me tightly as he kisses and fucks the hell out of me, not just tipping me over the edge, but pushing me with everything he's got.

I bear down, contracting around him as the orgasm consumes me. I've never felt anything this intense in my life.

I hear Levi moan, long and loud as he surrenders to his own release.

I don't want to move. I want to lie on top of him forever, soaking in his warmth, his breath, *everything*.

He calms me and speaks truth into me in a way no one ever has. No one's ever bothered to try.

"What is it?" His hand glides up and down my spine.

"I'm just happy." I sigh and kiss his jaw. "Like, this happiness might be illegal."

"I won't arrest you." He kisses my cheek before rolling us to our sides as he smiles in that mischievous way he does. "But that doesn't mean I won't use the handcuffs on you."

"Can we do that next?"

He laughs and pulls me to him. "Easy, girl. Let me recover

from last time first."

"Well, hurry up."

"I HAD NO idea that police departments had such nice facilities."

We're standing in the middle of a gym at his work, and Levi is squatting more weight than I've ever seen on a bar at one time.

He's so damn strong.

"It's easier to come here to work out before or after work." He's sweating as he sets the bar back on the rack. "While I rest, you can do leg presses. Come here."

He leads me to a machine and gets me ready to go, then watches me carefully as I complete three sets of ten presses, upping the weight with each set.

My legs are strong, but I feel the strain.

While I rest, he goes back to squats. And so the next hour goes, alternating between sets, with him taking a turn, and then watching me closely as I take mine.

He's actually super sexy when his hand finds my ass as he leads me from each piece of machinery.

"I don't usually lift weights," I admit as I stretch out my legs. "I do a ton of cardio and yoga, but I don't always have the equipment or time to do weights."

"You should," he says as he sets his dumbbells down and smiles at me. "It'll help your cardio, as well."

"Your arms are *so damn hot* when they're full of blood."

I bite my lip, looking Levi up and down, and then run to him, hopping up into his arms and wrapping my legs around his hips. He catches me easily.

"Stay where you are." He reaches for his phone, turns on the camera, and points it to the mirror, taking a picture of us. I don't smile for the camera. Instead, I kiss his cheek as he looks at the lens.

"I want a copy."

"Yeah?"

"Of course."

"Then you'd better do another set of leg presses."

"You're a hard-ass."

He laughs and walks to the machine. "You're the one who wanted to come with me today, sweetheart. Let's do this."

FOR THE LOVE of all that's holy, I'm *so sore*.

It's been twenty-four hours since we left the gym, and every muscle in my legs and ass is screaming in pain. I can barely walk. I had to climb the stairs to my bedroom about an hour ago, and I thought I was going to die.

But now, I'm standing in the downstairs bathroom, staring at the toilet. I can't do this. There is no way in hell I can sit down. My legs are like a baby's. Weak. Pathetic.

"This is going to suck," I groan.

"Are you okay in there?" Levi starts to open the door, but I lean over and slam it shut.

"I'm fine."

"I heard you moan. Are you sick?"

I roll my eyes and blow a strand of hair out of my eyes. "No, I'm not sick. I'm *sore*. And I don't know how I'm going to sit down to use the bathroom."

He chuckles, and I begin to plan his demise.

He's a sadist. That's the only explanation for working me so hard that I can barely move.

"So glad you find this funny!"

"Let me in, and I'll help you sit down."

"Not a chance in hell. We have *not* been seeing each other long enough for you to join me in the bathroom. I can do it. Go away."

"I can stay out here in case you need me."

"Go away," I repeat, and then listen for his footsteps leading away from the door. I turn back to the toilet and sigh. "This is going to suck. But I have to pee *so bad*."

So I lift my sundress, pull my panties down, and hold onto the vanity as I lower myself down.

About halfway, I have to just fall. Let all the muscles go and *fall*. Because it's agony otherwise.

I do my business, and when I'm done, standing up isn't nearly as bad as lowering down. Thank God.

Once I've washed up, I open the door and shriek at Levi.

"I told you to leave!"

"I had to stay in case you fell." He hooks a piece of hair behind my ear. "You're so cute when you're sore."

"Eff that." I push past him to the kitchen. "My *ass* hurts, Levi. Muscles I didn't know I had are sore."

"Okay, let's do this." He lifts me easily and carries me up the stairs, through the bedroom to the bathroom.

"I don't have to use the bathroom anymore."

Without a word, he fills the tub with hot water, and after he digs around under the sink, he finds some Epsom salts and pours a generous amount into the water.

He turns to help me take off my clothes, but I shake my head.

"I can do this."

When I'm naked, and the tub is full, Levi helps me down into the water, and I let out a long, grateful sigh.

"Oh, this feels nice."

"Soak for about twenty minutes," he says. "Do you want some tea?"

"Yes, please."

He nods and hurries out of the room, and I sit back and let the water and salts do their job. I feel better already.

My live shows are incredibly physical. I fly on wires and do aerial work. I dance my ass off. But none of that has ever made me feel this sore.

I move my legs up and down, stretching my calves in the hot water. Before long, Levi returns with a steaming mug.

"How's it going?"

"It's nice," I admit and take the tea. "My legs feel better already."

"Good. We'll put you in another bath like this before bed. You should be much better by tomorrow."

"I hope so. I want to go to the studio tomorrow."

"Does that mean you don't want to go with me to the gym again in the morning?"

I narrow my eyes at him. "Hell, no. No way. You hurt me there."

"It's good for you."

"Nope. I'd rather let Jax throw me on my ass."

"That doesn't sound fun to me either."

"At least I can sit on the toilet unassisted the next day," I say with a laugh. "But I will admit, I'm not as in shape as I thought I was."

"You're in excellent shape. It's a different *kind* of shape. It's okay that you're not a muscle head."

"Hey, you didn't send me our picture."

"Oh, right." He pulls his phone out of his pocket and taps the screen. "Sent."

"Can I see it?"

He turns the screen to me, and I smile. "You're so handsome. And buff. Look at those arms holding me up."

"You're just with me for my strong arms."

"All the better for you to hold me with."

"So I should continue working out?"

"Yes, please."

"So noted." He laughs and stands to leave the bathroom.

"Wait. How am I going to get out of here?"

"That sore, huh?"

"It hurts my pride to admit it, but yes."

"Come on." He holds his hand out for mine, and then pulls me to my feet, his eyes pinned to my body as he watches the water sluice down my torso.

"Like what you see?"

Without answering, he lifts me over his shoulder and carries me to the bedroom, not concerned in the least about the trail of water he's leaving behind us.

"You're getting everything wet!"

"I'm only interested in getting *you* wet." He tosses me on

the bed and starts stripping out of his own clothes. "Let's see if we can rub those muscles and make them better."

"Wrong muscles, loverboy."

"Let's just try anyway."

eleven

Levi

I stretch and reach over to pull Starla into my arms. We start every night tangled together, but ultimately end up rolling away.

But when I reach over, I'm met with cold bed sheets.

No Starla.

I crack an eye and glance around. The room is bathed in grey light, the first signs of morning just starting to peek through.

She must be downstairs working. Most nights, she sleeps fine through the night, but once in a while, insomnia hits her. When it does, she usually goes to fool around on her piano.

I pad downstairs, but there's no sound coming from the living room. No smells from the kitchen.

"Starla?"

I prop my hands on my hips and listen.

Nothing.

"What the hell?" I hurry back upstairs, my heart starting to pound in my chest with worry. I reach for my phone and dial her number.

"Good morning," she says.

"Where are you?"

"I'm taking a walk by the waterfront. You were sleeping so peacefully, I didn't want to disturb you."

"Are you near Lady Liberty?"

"About a hundred yards, yeah."

"Stay where you are."

Before she can answer, I hang up and reach for a pair of shorts and a tank, then hurry out of the house, jogging down to the waterfront.

It's not far. I glance up and down the sidewalk and see her sitting on a bench not far from the monument.

She smiles at me as I hurry to her, then frowns when she sees my face.

"What's wrong? Did something happen?" she asks.

"Yeah, I woke up, and you were gone." I pull her in for a hug. "Don't do that to me. If you want to walk, just wake me up and say so."

"You were sleeping," she reminds me, frowning up at me. She sets off down the sidewalk, and I fall into step beside her. "I am a grown woman, and I'm allowed to walk whenever I want."

"You have a stalker." I take her hand in mine and hold on tight.

"I haven't heard a peep out of them in more than a week. It was probably a random weirdo."

"Maybe. Maybe not. Please just humor me and let me walk with you."

"Fine." She sighs as if she's picking her battles, and we walk in silence for several minutes. "It's quiet down here this early. I haven't seen a soul."

Something in her voice sounds . . . sad.

"Are you okay?"

"Sure. Why do you ask?"

"I don't know, you just seem lost in thought."

"Maybe I am." She sighs again. "Today's my mom's birthday."

"Oh? You should call and wish her a happy birthday."

She shakes her head, looking out at the first ferry of the morning making its way across the Sound.

"I wouldn't even know how to reach her. I don't have her number."

She glances up at me and then back out at the water.

"I could probably find it if you want."

"Nope." She leads us to a bench and sits, watching the ferry. "I don't want it."

"Why not?"

She glances at me again, her eyes searching my face.

"I haven't spoken to her or anyone else in my family in more than fifteen years. I was never close to my mom, and it's really okay. There are just moments, like on her birthday, that I wish it were different."

"I wish it was different for you, too." I lean over and kiss her temple. "I don't know what I'd do without my family."

"I have a family," she insists. "I have Jax and Meredith. And my assistant, Rachel. There are people in my life that I love. Family doesn't always come from blood."

I love you.

I don't say the words out loud. Instead, I smile at her.

"You're right. I've learned that since our family has been absorbed by the Montgomerys. They're a huge, close family, and not all of them are blood. In fact, I have a feeling Gail Montgomery would yank my ear off if I suggested otherwise."

"Oh, she would," Starla says with a laugh. "Gail is fiercely protective of her family. *All* of them. So, I have people in my life. I don't *need* the ones I was born to."

"I can see that."

Just then, my phone rings in my pocket.

"It's Joy." I frown as I accept the call. "Hello."

"Hey, favorite brother-in-law."

"What do you want?" I ask with a chuckle.

"I need some help at the clinic. You're handy. Jace is at work. Can you come help me?"

"Why don't you call a professional?"

"Because I have a handy brother-in-law. Please?"

"Yeah, give me about an hour, and I'll be there."

"Great, thanks."

She hangs up, and I look over at Starla. "Joy needs help."

"I heard. I guess we should head back to the house."

We stand, and I turn to the sidewalk just as Starla jumps onto my back.

"Carry me!"

"You said you wanted to take a walk."

"My legs still hurt."

"That was a week ago, sweetheart."

"I don't care. Just carry me."

I laugh, hop a little to get her settled better on my back, and then set off to the house. It's a good workout for me, and by the time we get there, I'm a sweaty, panting mess.

"Wow, I wasn't going to make you carry me the whole way, but you were fast."

"Good workout," I reply as I set her down and take the steps three at a time, reaching the bedroom before her. "I wonder what Joy needs at the clinic?"

"I guess you'll see soon enough."

"We'll both see. You're coming with me."

She smiles. "Yay! I love animals. Maybe she has puppies I can kiss on."

"You can kiss on me."

"You're not a puppy. Take me to the puppies."

"HI, PRETTY LADY."

Starla glances around in surprise as we walk into Joy's veterinary clinic. There's no one else in the lobby.

I know who's talking; it's just fun to watch Starla try to figure it out.

Bill whistles a long catcall, making Starla laugh.

"What the heck?"

I point to the African grey parrot sitting on the file cabinet behind the desk.

"Hi, Bill," I say.

"Fuck off," Bill says but eyes Starla. "Pretty lady."

"Well, hello, handsome bird," Starla croons. "How are you?"

"Shitty day," he says and shifts back and forth on his feet. "Shitty day."

"Well, hopefully, it'll get better," Starla says as Joy comes walking out. "Your parrot is awesome."

"Hey, guys. He has a bit of a potty mouth, but he's a staple here now. Good boy, Bill. Come on back."

We follow Joy through the doors to the area of the clinic that most people don't get to see. Cages of all different sizes line one wall, most containing cats and dogs that Joy and the other vets are treating.

"I love animals," Starla says with excitement. "Your job is so cool."

"Thank you," Joy says. "Come on into my office."

"What do you need fixed?" I ask her.

"Oh, nothing." She reaches into a bed and takes out the kitten she's been nursing. "You haven't checked on your kitten in a while. She misses you."

"Wait. We're getting a *kitten*?"

Starla dances in place and reaches out for the baby, cradling it against her face.

I'm stuck on the *we*. *We're* getting a kitten.

"I told Levi he needs to adopt her," Joy says. "He needs something to love."

"I have plenty of love," I object, but Starla is already kissing and hugging the little feline.

"Oh, you're the most precious cat to ever be born, aren't you? *Baby mine . . .*"

"She's singing a lullaby," I inform Joy, who just smirks at me. "You did this on purpose."

"She needs a home," Joy says. "And you'll give her a good one. She's the sweetest thing."

"Yes, she is," Starla says, kissing the baby's cheek, then lets it nuzzle down against her neck. "Look, she's already attached to me. I'm her mommy."

"Christ." I rub my eyes and then glare at Joy for the ambush.

"She can't go home for another four weeks or so," Joy

says as she reaches out to pet the kitten. "She still has some growing to do."

"She's so sweet," Starla says. "I'll name her Felicity Mae."

"Oh, what a precious name," Joy says with a grin. "I'll start calling her that now. Do you want to see some puppies?"

"YES!"

"No," I say at the same time, shaking my head. "Hell, no. She'll want one of those, too, and that's a hard *no*."

"Why do you hate fun?" Starla demands, passing the sleeping kitten back to Joy. "I'm not taking one home, I'm just going to enjoy them for a minute. Don't kill my thunder."

"Come on," Joy says, leading us out of the office and back to the main animal area. She opens a cage, and six lab puppies come lumbering out and straight to Starla, who just sits on the floor and opens her arms wide.

"Oh my goodness," she breathes. She pulls two in for kisses, while the others climb over her and nibble on her jeans. "This is what heaven looks like. This is it."

"They're cute," I concede, but narrow my eyes at Joy. "And I'm not taking any of them."

"They're all spoken for," she says with a laugh. "But who doesn't like playing with a whole herd of puppies?"

"I sure do," Starla says with a laugh as she tumbles backwards, three puppies all trying to lick her face at the same time. "Oh, Lord, this is the best way to start the day. We should do this every day."

"I'll stick with coffee," I say, but can't help but laugh as the puppies continue playing with her. They *are* funny. "I hate to break up this lovefest, but I have to go to work."

"Fine." Starla sits up and sighs, but the puppies attack again, and she falls onto her back in a fit of giggles and sloppy puppy kisses. "Give me a minute."

"I HAVE TO work tonight," Starla says with a frown two days later. I just arrived at her house after work and brought Caesar salads with blackened chicken from Salty's with me for dinner.

"What kind of work?" I take a bite of my salad and decide it needs more lemon, so I squirt some on top.

"Fan mail." She swallows a piece of chicken and takes a drink of water. "I have so much of it piled up, and I'll have another delivery next week. I need to get caught up."

"People still send actual letters?"

"Some, yeah. Or cards. Gifts. It's nice of them, and I want to read it myself, so my publicist's office sends me a weekly box. If there's not much to send, they'll wait a week or two."

"Interesting. Okay, I'll help."

"You don't have to do that."

"It'll be fun. Where are they?"

She shoves a big bite of salad into her mouth and walks to a spare bedroom, coming back with the biggest-sized flat rate mailing box in her arms. She sets it down on the floor between us and then sits in her chair, her feet pulled up under her.

"That's them."

"Okay, as we read, I suggest we make piles, sorting them out. We'll do one for things you want to respond to, another for gifts, and a third for miscellaneous."

"You're ridiculously organized," she says.

"You're welcome." I wink and reach for an envelope. There's

a card inside. "It says *Just a note to make your day brighter.*" I flip it open and then snap it shut again.

"What is it?"

"A dick pic." I throw the card on the floor outside of the box. "That's the trash pile."

"Okay, that's funny."

"Not funny." I take a bite of chicken. "Let's wait to look through the rest until *after* I'm done eating. Just in case."

"Good idea." She eyes the card on the floor. "Was it at least a *good* dick pic?"

"Does that exist?"

"I mean, if you were to send me one, it would be a good one."

"It's not my dick, and I won't ever be sending you a photo of it. You can just see it in real life."

She's giggling now, holding her sides with the hilarity of it all.

"I don't understand the *dick pic.* Do men really think we want to see that? Are y'all so proud of what God gave you that you can't help yourselves from showing it off? Because I have to tell you, as a female, we *do not* want photos of your penis. I enjoy your penis, and I still don't want a keepsake photo of it. Dicks aren't the most attractive part of the male anatomy."

"I'm uncomfortable with this conversation." I shift in my seat and frown at my salad. "I don't send pictures of myself naked."

"Oh, men don't even have to be naked to send them. All they do is just whip them out and snap a photo. It's disgusting."

"How often do you receive them?"

"Daily."

I choke on my lettuce and have to take a drink of water. "*Daily?*"

"Oh, yeah. It's a common occurrence. And I'd bet women who aren't famous get them on the regular, too. Men are just . . . proud. And it's baffling."

"I can't say that I know anyone who does that." I shake my head as Starla shoves her empty salad aside and wipes her mouth.

"Okay, let's get this over with."

She pulls out a letter and reads it, then smiles as she tucks it back into the envelope and sets it aside. "This is the keep pile."

"What did it say?"

"It was from a young girl who said she enjoys my songs. She was very sweet. Those are my favorites. They just sound so innocent."

We both reach for more mail, and over the next half hour, we read a wide array of messages, everything from the usual *you're my favorite artist* to a marriage proposal that joined the trash pile.

"Come on, he was handsome," Starla says, laughing her ass off.

"I'm so glad you're finding the humor in this."

"I had no idea that proposals and dick pics from strangers would make you so jealous."

"*Six* dick pics," I remind her. "In this box alone. What the fuck is wrong with people?"

"Proud," she says again. "So damn proud."

"I guess." I reach for a bigger envelope and pull out a typed letter and a picture. Starla's reading something else, and I don't alert her to what's in my hands.

Not yet.

The photo is of the two of us at the restaurant, sitting in the booth, before the rude waitress approached.

The image has been altered to look like we've both had our necks slashed, with blood coming out of our mouths, dripping onto the table.

I set it face-down on the table and read the letter.

Dear cunt,

God, I fucking hate you. Look at you, just out there living your life as if you shouldn't feel guilty for anything. As if you're innocent.

We both know you're not innocent, you stupid bitch.

And I'm going to make you pay.

Looks like you have someone who means something to you now. I'll make him pay, too. Before I kill you slowly. I'll torture him, right in front of your eyes so you can feel what I felt. It's all your fault.

Soon.

Rage. Blinding, boiling rage is all I feel as I set the letter face-down over the photo and take a long, deep breath.

"Levi?"

"Give me a minute. Don't touch this."

I stand and walk to the back door, staring through the glass to the pool in the back yard. I need a second to reel in my emotions. I want to *kill* whoever sent this. I want five minutes alone with them so I can tear them limb from limb.

"Levi, talk to me."

I turn to find her standing behind me, wringing her hands at her waist.

"You need to read this."

I walk back to the table and retrieve the letter. Starla takes it from me, and her eyes scan the page, getting wider the longer she reads.

"My God." She covers her mouth and reads it again. "What the hell?"

"There's a photo."

She looks up at me as a tear falls from the corner of her eye. "Let me see."

I want to say no. I want to shield her from this bullshit. But she *needs* to see it, so I pass it to her.

With one glance, she drops it to the floor and runs for the bathroom, heaving into the toilet.

I hurry after her and rub her back, then wet a washrag with cold water and press it to the back of her neck.

"Easy, baby."

"I don't understand," she murmurs, reaching for the rag and wiping it over her face, her mouth. "What in the hell is happening?"

"Clearly, someone is pissed at you."

I take the rag from her and rinse it, then wipe it over her forehead, her cheeks. When she's calmed down, we walk back to the table. I retrieve the letter and photo and set them face-down on the surface again.

"It's not nothing," I say.

"No." She swallows. "It's not."

"I'll take this to the station tonight. But first, I want to ask you, have you wronged anyone so horribly that they could want to hurt you?"

She frowns at me. "Of course, not. I haven't fired anyone. I haven't done *anything*. I have no idea what this is about."

"I didn't think so, but I had to ask. Also, this is a good time to address your security team. Or the lack thereof."

"What about them?"

"I wasn't impressed after the show a couple months ago. They let too many people touch you."

"They do a fine job."

"They're not here now."

She scowls. "Of course, not. I'm not working, remember? I don't want them with me for the day-to-day."

"Not even now?"

"You have a car parked outside my house twenty-four-seven. That's plenty."

I sigh and rub my hand down my face. "Here's the thing, Starla. I'm not convinced it's plenty. Not after this. So, for the foreseeable future, you won't ever be alone. If I can't be with you, Jax or Meredith will be."

"I'm a prisoner."

"You're a person we all care about, and we're going to take care of you," I counter. "I'm going to find out who this sick bastard is, and we'll put an end to this. But in the meantime, you're not alone. That's non-negotiable."

"Fine."

"And I'm moving in here."

She cocks a brow. "Gee, you're so romantic."

"This isn't how I intended to tell you we're moving in together, but it is what it is."

She blinks rapidly. "You mean you were going to *ask* me?"

"No, that's not what I meant." I take her hand and kiss her thumb. "Besides, *we've* already adopted a kitten. Did you think we'd be sharing custody?"

A slow smile spreads over her gorgeous face. "How sweet. We're fur-parents."

"Funny. Never alone, you understand?"

"Yes, sir." Her mouth is sassy, but she climbs into my lap and lays her head on my shoulder. "Why do people suck?"

"That's the question of the year."

twelve

Starla

He's comforting me. I'm trying to pretend that it doesn't bother me, that the upchucking in the toilet was just because of the graphic content of the photo, but the whole situation is starting to freak me the fuck out.

I just don't want to lose my freedom. I'm independent, almost to a fault.

Obviously.

"You should think about warning your family," Levi says as his hand rubs up and down my back.

"I'll call Jax and Mer in just a bit."

"No." He kisses my temple. "Your biological family. *You* may not want to have much to do with them, but a good stalker will try to find ways to hurt you, and they will threaten your family, too."

"There's really no way anyone could trace me to my family." I lean back and look him in the eyes. "And I'm not saying that just because I don't want to talk to them. My legal name isn't tied to theirs. I have never spoken about my family to anyone, personally or publicly, except for Mer and Jax, and they aren't telling anyone. If I thought they were in danger, I would contact them, but I don't believe they are."

"What the hell, Star? What's the backstory here?"

I sigh and lay my head on his shoulder again. I should talk to him about them. I know that.

I just hate it. I *never* discuss them. I haven't said their names in more than fifteen years.

But Levi's different. Whatever we have here—and if I'd stop being so damn stubborn, I'd admit that it's love—is important to me, and I don't want secrets with him. I would be hurt if the tables were turned.

"You know those cults, mostly in the south, where people hold snakes in *church,* and it's all fire and brimstone and stuff?"

"I've seen news reports about it."

"Well, I've seen it up close and personal. It's not a real church. They say they're Christians, but what I grew up in wasn't that. It was horrible and evil. It was the worst extreme you can think of, times a hundred."

I move from his lap to my chair facing him and push my hair up into a bun, using the hair tie I keep on my wrist.

"My father is the high priest. That's what he calls himself. Sometimes, he's the bishop. I think it just depends on his mood.

"They would bring snakes, venomous ones, into church every month. Sometimes, people would get bit and die. It was a freak show. Not to mention, I was required to get up at four every morning to memorize bible verses until it was time for schoolwork. We weren't allowed to go to regular school. And it wasn't normal homeschool either. My parents felt that both of those things were full of Satan, so they taught us at home. I learned to read by reading the bible."

"Lovely," Levi says and rubs his fingers over his mouth. "How many siblings do you have?"

"Nine."

His head snaps up in surprise. *"Nine?"*

"There are ten of us altogether, but I'm the only one who left. I was always the rebellious one. I listened to radio stations that weren't allowed. I cut off all my hair myself, ruining blond hair that went to my ass. I liked breaking the rules because I thought they were ridiculous.

"And I was punished."

"Punished how?"

I raise my shirt and turn to the side, not able to look him in the eye. "These scars?"

"I've felt them," he confirms softly.

"Whip marks."

"Are you fucking kidding me?"

I shake my head. "No. I've thought about covering them with a tattoo, but I don't know what I want. Punishments included whippings, starvation, having to walk around naked for days. You name it. They always said it was God's will that they punish me like that."

"Assholes."

"For sure. I don't have any idea how they came to be that way. I don't know if my father was just a psychopath and brainwashed my mother. I don't even know who my grandparents are.

"There were about forty people in the *church*. Twelve of

those were our family. It was like being in prison. It was awful. So, when I turned eighteen, I packed a change of clothes and ran away.

"I went to LA, and I had to lie on job applications just so I could get some work to have money. I waited tables, I cleaned hotel rooms. Anything. One of the hotels was the Roosevelt, and I was singing in the hallway by my cart one morning. Donald, my manager, heard me and asked me if I'd come to LA to try to be a singer.

"I told him that I came to LA to find a life. It was really that simple. And that's the last day I ever woke up wondering how I was going to eat or pay the rent. Donald took me in and helped me form a career that most people only dream of."

"Good for you," Levi says and reaches over to take my hand in his. "Now I understand why you don't have any contact with them."

"I do send them money."

"What?" His voice is utterly calm, but every muscle contracts.

"I do." I shrug a shoulder. "About a year after the music took off, I had a private investigator look into them. They never filed a missing person's report on me. Ever. Because I also didn't have a birth certificate. According to the county, I'd never been born. Which explains why no one came to find out why my siblings and I weren't in school.

"When I was in LA and changed my name, I had to forge an original birth certificate. Anyway, they were still doing their thing, living in squalor. They'd had another baby. And all I could think was, those kids deserve *something*. I'm never going back there to physically help them. I can't. But I did have the investigator call CPS to report the family, and I send money in the oldest siblings' names, for them to help the others.

"They had to sign legal papers that state they can't give money to the church. They can't help our parents. It's for the kids. And I don't send it directly. It goes through my financial people, so I'm very hands-off."

"None of them have left? Gone to look for you?"

"Not that I'm aware of."

"Star, could this stalker *be* one of them?"

That brings me up short. I blink, staring at Levi. Is it possible? I suppose it is. The older kids know who I am.

"It's not *im*possible," I concede, speaking slowly. "But they receive a *lot* of money, Levi. I can't imagine they'd want—"

"If they're angry at you for leaving, or for being a celebrity, or *anything*, they could do it. If they have mental health issues like your parents . . ."

"I hadn't thought of that. I guess I could call my investigator and have him peek in on them. He does every couple years or so."

"Give me his name," Levi says, opening his phone. "I'll call him."

I should bristle at that. Eddie is under *my* employ, and he's always been excellent at maintaining confidentiality. But the idea of taking another step back from my family is too enticing to throw away.

I open my phone, find Eddie's info, and send it to Levi.

"There you go. We can call him together tomorrow, and I'll let him know it's okay to work directly with you."

"It's in my calendar," Levi confirms. "If it comes down to telling them what's going on here—"

"It won't." I cut him off and cross my arms over my chest. "Trust me, they *don't care.* And I know it's not about them anyway. This has been going on for a long time, and they've never mentioned my family."

Levi doesn't meet my eyes as he carefully sets his phone down, then links his fingers together and leans on the table.

"Excuse me?"

I swallow. Shit.

"Starla."

"I've been getting emails for a few months."

"How many months?"

"Six? Eight?"

"Christ." He stands and paces around the kitchen. "You didn't think it was a good idea to tell me?"

"They weren't threatening until very recently. Just . . . weird. And I've never received photos like this until the one you saw of me and Meredith."

"I can't protect you if I don't know everything."

"Well, now you do." I stand and prop my hands on my hips. "You saw the dick pics in this box. The proposal. This isn't even a *fraction* of the shit that happens on Instagram. The shit that comes through the public email address. People are *disgusting*, Levi, and I've learned to filter out most of it. I ignore it."

"So, these emails are coming to your personal account."

"Yeah, but any decent hacker could probably find it." I shrug. "I mean, I would think. I really didn't think it was a big deal."

"It's a big deal," he replies and paces away from me. "That night that I didn't come here after work? Remember?"

"Yes."

"I'd been working a stalker case. The girl was obsessed with this guy. He was married, had kids. Didn't want anything to do with her. She was crazy. So, we arrested her for harassment, and I told him to get a restraining order."

He looks outside again.

"That morning I left, I got a call from Matt. He was at the guy's residence and thought I should come since I was working the case. I got there . . ." He shakes his head. "I got there, and the guy's wife was dead. Stabbed. I won't describe the rest of it to you because I still can't get it out of my head. It haunts me."

He turns to me.

"The stalker was dead, too. The guy came home from work and found the stalker slicing up his wife. Shot her in the head. My point is, *the wife's dead*, Starla. She's dead because her husband didn't think it was a big deal and didn't report anything to the police until it had gone too far. Your life is too precious to fuck around with this."

"I'm sorry." I wrap my arms around his middle and press my face to his chest. "I'm so sorry you went through that."

"Bad days happen," he reminds me. "And I'll be damned if I let that happen to you. It's a big deal, and we're going to get to the bottom of this."

"Maybe it's all for show?" But we both know it's not.

"Maybe." He sighs. "Grab your laptop. We're going to the office. I want my tech guys to look this over, and not just through a forwarded message. I'm also taking the letter on the table for prints. They might be able to find something on it.

"What scares me the most is that they're following you. They followed you shopping with Meredith, and us out for dinner. I haven't seen anything suspicious."

"I haven't felt like I'm being watched." I rub my hands up

and down my arms. "Until now. Now, I'm creeped out."

"That makes two of us," he mutters. "Come on. Let's do this."

⌒

"THIS IS NO big deal," Levi says two days later. He's leaning against the doorjamb of my bathroom, watching me primp. "They're going to love you."

"I'm meeting your *parents*." I stare at him in the mirror as I hold my curling iron, waiting for my hair to curl. "Of course, it's a big deal. I could just stay here while you go celebrate your dad's birthday."

"No." He shakes his head and walks up behind me. His hands glide from my hips, move up my sides, and cup my breasts. "You're not allowed to be alone."

"There are two cops outside now."

"No way." He kisses my neck, and when he pulls away, I let the curl out. "You already know everyone there."

"Except your parents." I shake my fingers through my hair, smooth on some lip gloss, and then turn out the bathroom light. "Okay. I guess I'm ready."

"You're gorgeous."

"I'm nervous." I shrug a shoulder. "And I never get nervous."

Once we're in Levi's car and on the road, I glance in the side mirror.

"Your guys are following us."

"They're following orders," he confirms. "Another guy will go watch the house while we're gone. Just in case."

"I would say this is too much, but I don't think it is."

"Did you get another email?"

"How would I know? You made me give the guy at the office my password, and I'm not allowed to use it."

"You opened a new email," he points out, and I roll my eyes.

He pulls into his parents' driveway and cuts the engine, but rather than getting out of the car, he rubs his palms up and down his thighs.

"I thought you said there was nothing to be nervous about?"

He smiles at me. God, he makes butterflies take flight in my belly.

"I've never brought a girl home before."

Before I can answer, he hops out of the car and hurries around to open my door.

I'm staring at him with a dropped jaw.

"What?" he asks.

"Never?"

"Never."

He takes my hand and leads me to the front door. He walks inside without knocking.

"Hey, girl," Lia says with a smile. "Come on in. I already made you a lemon-drop martini."

"I don't usually drink," I say but take the glass from her. "But I'll have just one. For courage."

"You're going to be great," she whispers before Levi leads me through the spacious house to the kitchen.

"Mom, Dad, this is Starla."

"Oh." Levi's mom stares at me in surprise, and then a huge smile breaks out over her face as she hurries over to hug me. "Well, hello."

"Hi."

I don't know if I've ever been hugged this tightly. I might lose all lung capacity if she doesn't let go soon.

"I'm Melody," she says when she finally pulls away. "And this is my husband, Linus."

"You're the birthday boy," I say when I reach out to shake his hand, but I'm pulled in for another hug. This one is gentle. Linus is a big man, like his sons. But where Levi has salt-and-pepper hair, Linus's is all white.

"That's me," he says with a kind smile.

"What can I do to help?" I glance around and stop cold. Levi's mom isn't cooking.

"Absolutely nothing," Melody says. "As you can see, Linus requested pizza for dinner."

"Cheeseburger pizza," Linus says with a wink. "But there's other stuff here if you'd rather."

"Are you kidding? Cheeseburger pizza is my jam."

And just like that, all of my nerves are gone. Levi's parents are warm. Kind. Much like their son.

When we all have full plates, we settle into the informal family dining room. The boys are chatting, drinking beer and giving each other shit about nearly *everything*.

"I'm Mom's favorite," Jace says with a simple shrug. "It's really that easy."

"In your dreams." Wyatt glares at his brother. "She tolerates you at best."

"I love all of my children equally," Melody says with a sigh. "Every time. We go through this every time."

"No one ever argues over my love," Linus says, and I smile at him.

"I think I'm your favorite," I tell him, and laugh when he

winks and holds his fist out for a bump.

"That you are, darling."

I think I might have a little crush on Levi's dad. Not in a weird, fetishy way. But in a he's-a-cool-dad way.

I smile smugly at Levi just as my phone rings.

"I'm sorry, everyone. This is Donald." I turn to Levi. "I have to take it."

"Absolutely," he says as I accept the call and step away from the table and into the living room. "Hi, Donald."

"How's my favorite girl?"

I smile, thinking of the conversation happening at the table.

"I'm good. How are you?"

"I'm great. Just calling to let you know that *20/20* wants to do a show with you. It'll be Diane Dobson doing the interview. This is big, baby. Primetime TV."

"Sounds like fun, actually."

"Perfect. They want to do the interview at your home in LA on Friday."

"Of *this* week? That's fast."

"That's what they want. So get your sexy ass to LA by Friday."

"Uh, Donald, I'm not coming to LA right now." I bite my lip, seeing *the look* Donald gives me whenever I dare to tell him no.

"Did you not hear the part about Primetime TV?"

"I did, and I'm happy to do it, it'll just have to be in Seattle." He's quiet for a moment. "Please."

"I'll see to it, and email you with the specifics."

"Here, let me give you my new email address." I rattle it off to him.

"Why the new address?"

"Too much spam in the other one," I lie easily.

"Okay. I'll be in touch."

He hangs up, and I sigh. I hope Nat and Luke don't mind me having the interview in their house. I know Luke is intensely private. I'll have to talk with them about it.

When I return to the dining room, everyone is pretty much done with their pizza, and there's a cake sitting in front of Linus with six candles lit.

"Now, we can sing," Melody says, leading the birthday song. When we're finished, Linus squeezes his eyes shut as if he's making a wish, and then blows out the candles.

"What did you wish for?" Joy asks.

"For Starla to sing with me in the living room after we eat this cake."

All eyes turn to me. "Really?"

"If you're up for it," Linus replies.

"Sure, that would be fun."

Linus shocks the hell out of me.

After dessert, we're in the living room, and Linus has an old guitar on his knee. He begins playing the opening notes of *Fire and Rain* by James Taylor, and I join him, singing harmony to his melody.

"How did you know that's one of my favorite songs?" I ask when we're finished.

"Because you're my favorite," he says with a wink.

thirteen

Starla

I don't know why I'm nervous.

Nat and Luke have been my friends for a long time. Luke is in the business. They'll understand.

Or, if they don't, I'll just rent a suite at a hotel for the interview. Either way, it'll work out.

I knock on the door, and Natalie answers it, holding a baby on her shoulder.

"Hey, Starla, come on in."

"Thanks." I close the door behind me and follow Nat to the large living room off the kitchen.

"Livvy's in school, and the others are napping. I just finished feeding this little one, and she should be asleep soon."

"Can I hold her?"

Nat looks at me in surprise but then smiles. "Of course, you can."

She carefully lays the sleepy baby in my arms, and I sit in the rocking chair, looking down into green eyes. The girl's little fist closes around one of my fingers, as sure as if it was directly around my heart.

"Oh, you're a charmer, aren't you?"

"Just like her mama," Luke confirms as he walks into the room and scoops his wife into his arms, planting a passionate kiss on her. We're all used to Luke's blatant affection for his wife.

The baby's eyes are heavy, and as I rock her back and forth, she falls asleep, still gripping onto my finger.

"She's out," I whisper. "Is it okay if we still talk?"

"Of course," Nat says in her normal voice. "If we had to be perfectly quiet during every nap time, I'd never get anything done. She won't wake up. What's going on?"

"I need to run something by you." I brush my fingertips over the baby's soft hair. "I got a call from my manager last night."

I tell them about the phone call, and my reluctance to go to LA right now.

"Levi thinks I'm being followed, and I'm not convinced he's wrong. I mean, I don't think someone can follow me twenty-four-seven, but they have taken photos of me while out with friends. He has the cops watching me all the time. In fact, one of his officers drove me over here because I'm not supposed to be alone."

I look up, mortified. "Oh my gosh. I promise you, I haven't brought anything bad to your home. I swear, I don't think they're really following me all the time."

"This place has more security than Fort Knox," Natalie assures me.

"Are you asking if you can hold the interview at Nat's place?" Luke asks with a frown.

"Yeah. I am. And I know about your intense need for privacy, so if the answer's no, that's okay. Honest. I can rent out the penthouse at a hotel or something."

Nat and Luke exchange a glance. Natalie smiles in that serene way she has that never fails to put someone at ease.

"I don't have an issue with it as long as it's stated on-air that you're vacationing at the time of the interview, and no identifying images of the house are used," Luke says. "No shots of the front of the house."

"That won't be a problem." I smile down at the baby. "I would never do anything to hurt your family."

"We know," Nat says. "It'll be great. It's exciting that they want to interview you."

"I'm not sure why they do," I reply honestly. "Frankly, I'm not in the middle of a tour, I don't have a record dropping anytime soon. Hell, I'm not even in the studio. Although, I have some songs finished that I'd love to record, and I'm thinking of asking Leo if I can use his studio."

"Oh, I'm sure he'd let you," Nat says. "They're home for a while now. You should call Sam."

I stare at her and then laugh, trying not to be too loud so I don't wake the baby. "You do remember that there was that one time, back in the day, that Leo and I saw each other naked, right? I don't think Sam likes that, and I can't say that I blame her."

"Do you plan to be naked with him now?"

I hold Luke's gaze with my own. I know he's intensely protective of his sister, as it should be. "Of course, not. I have a feeling that Levi will be the last person to ever see me naked."

Natalie grins again. "That's the most romantic thing I've ever heard."

"You're kidding me, right?" Luke demands, making me laugh again. Luke's only the most romantic man ever born in the history of men.

"I mean, it's pretty romantic," I agree with a snort. "Leo's a great guy. A good musician. And four-thousand-percent married to Sam. I'm not interested in anything more than music."

"Say it just like that, and Sam won't have an issue," Luke says with confidence. "She's not stupid. Regarding the house, we're good there. We trust you."

"Thank you."

I don't know why I suddenly have tears in my eyes. It's ridiculous. I have an amazing life. There's no reason to cry.

Maybe it's the relief that these people that I care about and respect, trust me. Perhaps it's the stress of the stalker.

Maybe I'm about to start my period.

I don't know.

"I think you need a huckleberry treat," Nat announces as she stands from her seat. "I have some huckleberry delight in the fridge. Do you want a piece?"

"Yes." I swipe a tear away and smile at both of them. "Yes, that sounds amazing."

❧

"THERE ARE TOO many people coming in and out," Levi says for the third time. "It's a safety issue."

"This is a production crew," I repeat. "And I have security. I have you and Aaron."

I point at the security guard my company sent up. He's currently standing by the front door, looking down at his phone.

"Are you serious?" Levi asks. "They sent *one* guy, and he's not even paying attention."

A man walks through the front door carrying cables looped around his shoulder.

"He didn't even glance up," Levi says, pointing. "That dude could have been a murderer."

"Right." I pat his shoulder. "Calm down, tiger. There are at least twenty people around."

"Damn it," Aaron mumbles. "I can't believe that dude killed me."

"You're on the fucking job, and you're playing *video games*?" Levi says, stomping toward Aaron. "What the hell?"

"Who the fuck are you?" Aaron asks.

"Who am I? You *met* me, asshole. I'm Levi Crawford, SPD. And you're fired."

"I don't work for you, *asshole*," Aaron sneers. "You can't fire me."

The two men are in the middle of a stare down, and I simply roll my eyes and leave, headed up to the guest room where the production crew has set up hair and makeup.

Men are ridiculous.

"Hi, Starla, I'm Yvette. I'll be doing your hair and makeup today."

"Hi." I sit in the high director's chair and sigh. "It's blissfully quiet up here. I thought my boyfriend was going to murder that security guy down there."

"Well, the security guy is a dufus," Yvette says with a smile and pulls my hair back into a ponytail, exposing all of my face and neck. "I walked through four times before he asked me who I was."

"So they didn't send the valedictorian of the security class." I shrug a shoulder. "It'll be okay. This feels good. It's been a while since I've been in hair and makeup. I need a spa day. Maybe I'll do that this weekend."

"Good plan," Yvette says, spreading primer on my face. "I could use a facial too, now that you mention it."

Over the next half hour, we discuss our favorite spas in LA, and which treatments we prefer. Just when she gets my fake lashes applied, Levi walks through the door.

"Good timing. Makeup's done, so now we just have to do hair." My smile fades when I see his face. "What's wrong?"

"I had Aaron fired."

I sigh and close my eyes in defeat.

I'm dating an overbearing, overprotective cop.

"He was my *only* security, Levi." Yvette discreetly exits the room, closing the door behind her. "And just like you always remind me, I have a stalker. Now I don't have anyone here to protect me."

His brown eyes narrow as he leans into me, speaking low.

"I can protect you better with my eyes closed than that idiot. If you think anything's going to happen to you on my watch, you have another thing coming, sweetheart. He wasn't helping anything. He was a liability. I'll be sticking with you, and my guys are outside. We don't need him."

"I feel like I should be paying the Seattle Police Department for all of the man hours I'm taking away from law and order."

"I'm sure they wouldn't mind a generous donation." His lips twitch as he leans in closer. "I'm going to kiss you."

"Don't you dare!" Yvette yells from the other side of the door. "She looks perfect the way she is."

I giggle. "Yeah, keep your lips to yourself, Detective."

He presses his lips to my ear. "I'm going to do a lot more than kiss you as soon as all of these damn people leave."

"It's a date."

⟡

"IS THERE ANYTHING you don't want me to ask today?" Diane asks before we begin filming.

"I never talk about my family," I inform her. "Aside from that, we'll see how it goes."

Diane smiles. I've met her before. She's interviewed me at least a half-dozen times. "Fair enough."

"And, action."

"Good evening," Diane begins, staring right into the camera behind me. We're outside by the pool, both mic'd up, and there's a large boom mic over us. "I'm Diane Dobson, and tonight we have a special guest on *20/20*. I'm thrilled to be in Seattle, Washington, with the pop megastar, Starla. Thank you for letting us crash in on your vacation, Starla."

"Thanks for crashing," I reply. "I'm just happy you have sunny weather."

"It *is* a nice day," Diane says, but I can see in her eyes that the small talk is just to get me to relax. I've seen it dozens of times before. This isn't my first rodeo. "We thought this would be a good time to catch up with you since you're between tours and albums right now. You're usually a *very* busy woman."

"I do like to stay busy, yes."

"How is vacation going?"

"I have to be honest, relaxing doesn't come easy for me. And because I can take my job anywhere, I find myself working, even though I'm on a break."

"Working how?"

"Writing songs, mostly. I had my piano shipped up a few weeks ago, and I've had time to enjoy the artistic process of writing."

"You've stayed in excellent shape, if I may say so," Diane says.

"Thank you. Being active is a big part of my career. I enjoy tumbling through the air and dancing. Putting on an exciting show is important to me, so I do my best to stay in shape, even when I'm not actively touring."

"I've seen that show, and you're a crazy woman on that stage."

"Thank you."

"Will you play us some songs on that piano before we go?"

"I'd love to."

Diane looks down at her card.

"Do you mind if we get a little personal here?"

I cock my head to the side. "Let's get personal, Diane."

"Have you recovered from Rick's death?"

I take a deep breath and look up at the trees. "You know, grief is a journey, not a line in the sand. It's been a long journey, and while I will always mourn the loss of Rick, I can honestly say that I've healed a tremendous amount."

"Are you in contact at all with Rick's family?"

His family hated my guts.

But the smile stays in place.

I'm not sure why we're talking about this. Rick's death was

five years ago.

"Unfortunately, no. I think it was too painful."

"What was it that helped you heal from that loss?"

"Music." I smile. "Having people in my life who are incredibly supportive. And time, honestly."

"Good for you. I'm glad you're doing well."

"Thank you."

"Cut."

Diane sags in her seat as soon as the camera is turned off.

"What's this all about?" I ask her. "Why all the questions about Rick? He's been gone for a long time."

"Because next week is the fifth anniversary of his death." She looks at me and frowns. "Didn't your people tell you this episode is about remembering Rick?"

No. Because if they had, I wouldn't have done it, and it pisses me off that Donald left that out when he called.

I should have *known.*

"I must not have gotten the memo," I mutter.

"I'm sorry." Diane looks sincere as she frowns. "I really am. I would have talked with you more before the interview if I'd known."

"It'll be okay."

"Can I ask you some questions, off camera?"

"Sure."

Yvette comes over to powder our noses.

"Did you talk to him that morning, before the accident?"

"I did," I confirm with a tight nod. I don't trust Diane to keep our conversation confidential, so I'm especially conscious of my words.

"What was his mental state that day?"

"He was tired," I reply. "But aside from that, I think he was fine."

"Not angry or upset about anything?"

I smile, not willing in the least bit to confide in Diane about my last conversation with Rick.

"Not when he spoke with me," I reply. "So, what are we doing next?"

The director steps over, notes in his hand.

"We're going down to the waterfront to let you two take a walk and chat as if you're two friends who haven't seen each other in a long time. And then we'll come back inside, and you can sing some songs on the piano."

"Okay. Let's do it." I hop off the chair and smile at Levi. "But I don't want anyone to forget; no shots of the front of this house."

I already put any personal photos of the family away from prying eyes. I didn't just put them in a closet, I took them to Nat and Luke's house just to be safe.

People are nosy.

"ACTION!"

We're walking on the sidewalk along the waterfront. There are cameras in front of us and behind us, but Diane and I are just walking casually.

We both changed our clothes. It'll look like we've spent several days together.

"One of the things that your fans love about you is your

willingness to be accessible to them. You interact on social media, almost every day. Why is that so important to you?"

"Well, I gave up trying to fight social media a long time ago. And, yes, there are some pitfalls to having your life out there, exposed for all to see."

Like crazy-ass stalkers.

"But for the most part, it's fun to interact with fans. They're supportive and funny. So funny."

"Sometimes, they aren't nice," she reminds me.

"I think that's true in every walk of life. Sometimes, people aren't nice in real life either."

"You recently had a bit of a social media hiccup when a video surfaced of you and a man in a restaurant."

My face is neutral, my voice even.

But, man, I hate this conversation.

"Yeah, sometimes I think there are trolls who try to turn something simple into a big deal."

"So you're saying that wasn't a big deal."

"It really wasn't."

"The waitress sounded pretty horrible. I saw the video."

I nod. "She wasn't very gracious, but I really just wanted to leave. I didn't want a scene. I think the whole situation was blown out of proportion."

"Well, one of the things that's been especially talked about since that video is the guy you were with."

I can't help the smile that spreads over my lips.

"Ah, I see that smile. What can you tell us about him?"

"What if I said I didn't want to tell you anything about him?"

"Come on, Starla. We've all seen him. Give us a little something."

"It's new," I reply, looking up at Levi, who's behind the camera in front of us. "And it's going very well. That's all I'll say for now."

"No chance of him speaking with us on camera?"

I laugh and shake my head no. "Absolutely not."

fourteen

Levi

"**M**y ass has grown," Starla says. She's sitting next to me on the couch, her legs thrown over mine as she munches on popcorn. "I need to work on that."

"Your ass is fine."

Her interview is on television, and she's watching with rapt attention. She's been critiquing every movement, every word.

She's so damn hard on herself.

The interview is almost over, and they're showing Starla at the piano with Diane sitting next to her, listening to Starla sing. I could tell while watching the interview in person that Diane likes Starla. She was engaging, and the look in her eyes said *fan*.

But you just never know what the press is going to say or how they will spin a story. Starla's been a nervous wreck about it for days. I'm glad the interview is airing so she can stop worrying about it.

"As you can see, Starla is enjoying her vacation, her time away from the spotlight for just a little while. But I think she'll be ready to get back to work shortly."

"Such a great interview, Diane," her co-anchor, Marty Randall says. "Did she talk any more about Rick and his tragic death?"

"You know, Marty, we did talk a bit off camera. I could really get the sense that she still grieves for Rick deeply, and may even feel some guilt where his death is concerned."

"Really? How so?" Marty asks.

"Yeah, how so?" Starla asks, sitting up.

"Well, she mentioned that when she spoke to Rick the morning of his death, that he seemed tired and just not himself."

"I never said that."

Diane continues. "Perhaps they fought or had a disagreement, and Rick was angry when he got in that car."

"A lover's spat, perhaps?" Marty asks.

"We don't know, and frankly, Starla didn't say more than that. I can only speculate."

"A great loss to the world of sports, that's for sure," Marty replies with a grave nod before they go to a montage of photos of Rick, some with Starla, before fading to his dates of birth and death, and then ending the show.

"Fuckers," Starla mutters, pacing the living room. "They basically just accused me of killing him."

"Well, I don't know if they did *that*."

She looks over at me as if to say, *seriously?*

"Okay, they made it sound bad."

"Why do they always have to try to put words in my mouth?" she demands. "It's ridiculous. I never said that we fought. I simply said Rick seemed tired. And she just had to run off with it. Now we'll have more social media shit where people will post polls. *Do you think Starla caused Rick's death?"*

She reaches for her phone.

"I'm putting an end to this bullshit." She puts the phone on speaker and sits on the edge of the couch.

"I take it you just saw the spot," Donald says, his voice too chipper. "You did fantastic, sweet girl. Absolutely fantastic."

"Bullshit," Starla replies. "You suckered me into doing that interview and didn't give me all of the details because you *knew* I wouldn't want to do it."

"Well—"

"You do this to me *all the time*, Donald, and I'm done. Do you hear me? If it ever happens again, you're fired."

"Now you listen to me, you can't just—"

"Oh, I can. I know you think you've got me cornered with that contract, but I made sure my attorney arranged it so I wouldn't lose everything to you if we parted ways. I'm not threatening you, Donald. I care about you, and I am grateful to you, but if you think you can pull shit like this without consequences, you're wrong. It's disrespectful and hurtful."

"Everything I do is for the betterment of your career."

"I call bullshit," Starla counters. "You do it for ratings. No more ambushes. I either know everything going in with a complete list of questions, or I don't do it. End of."

"Fine. Go cool off."

Donald hangs up, and Starla tosses her phone on the coffee table.

"What a jerk," she whispers. "He will *not* guilt me into just blindly following him anymore. I'm not nineteen anymore, Levi. I'm too old for this shit, and I have a say in my damn life."

"Agreed."

She glances over at me, and her expression softens. She scoots over to lean into me and sighs.

"Well, that was a shitshow."

"Not really. It was a good interview. You looked great. They just added the bullshit at the end."

"My ass has grown," she pouts, making me laugh.

"Come with me to the gym, and we'll work on it."

"You try to kill me at the gym."

"I won't try to kill you." I kiss her hair. "You're beautiful the way you are. If you want to tighten up your ass, I can help you with that. I'm fine either way."

She snuggles closer. "Okay, you can help. But curb your sadistic tendencies. I don't want to be unable to sit for a week after."

"I'm not a sadist. But I do know people who are."

Her head whips up, her eyes widening. "Seriously?"

"Yeah. I'm not into dishing out pain. I'm a pleasure guy."

"You *are* good at the pleasure." She straddles my lap and kisses me deeply. "What should we do now?"

"What do you want to do?"

A smile spreads over her face. "I want to swim."

She jumps off my lap and runs for the backyard, stripping out of her clothes on the way, leaving a trail not unlike Hansel and Gretel. By the time I walk through the open sliding glass doors, she's already in the water, swimming easily across the pool.

I shuck out of my shoes and clothes and dive in with her, swimming beside her.

When we reach the end of the pool, I pull her to me and easily slip inside her.

"Well, shit," she says, leaning her head back against the side of the pool. "That feels good."

"Too good?"

She grins. "Never."

"HEY, CRAWFORD, I have something for you."

I glance up at Jim Parker, the IT cop I assigned to Starla's stalker, as he leans on the doorway to my office.

"Okay." I stand and follow him down the hall to his own office where he has several computers set up, along with Starla's laptop. "What's up?"

"I think I followed the stalker email back to the beginning." He sits in his chair, and I lean over his shoulder, watching as he wakes up Starla's computer. "It started over a year ago."

"A *year?*"

"As far as I can tell. I've printed them all out for you, and every single one comes from a different email address, but they're all the same tone. They're definitely written by the same person. Here's the first one."

It's your fault. Your fault that she's dead. You wouldn't help me. Why wouldn't you help me? I've always been there for you! Time and again, I've been there for you, but you were not there for me. For us. And now she's gone, and it's your fault. I can't believe you're such a heartless bitch.

There's no signature.

"It's not threatening," I say with a sigh.

"No, in fact, they weren't threatening for about six months. Some of these weren't even opened, so Starla probably hasn't seen them."

"Maybe she assumed they were spam?"

"She might have. But they escalate for sure, and it's absolutely the same person. When I try to trace it back to an IP address, I hit a dead end. I don't know how they managed to block it unless they're a talented programmer or hacker. We're still working on that."

He reaches to the other side of his desk and hands me a stack at least two inches thick of printed emails.

"This is them?"

"There are hundreds," he says. "And those are just the ones I found. I found a bunch in her trash bin, but there's a chance she's deleted some that I couldn't find."

"Thanks, man. Keep me posted."

"Will do."

I walk back to my office, set the emails on my desk, and sigh. "Jesus."

I spend the next two hours poring through them. Marty's right, they start calm. Sad. And then the tone turns angry. Psychotic. Sometimes, there are several in a day, and then other times, weeks pass between messages.

There's no rhyme or reason to the pattern.

I don't like that. I also don't like that we can't trace the fucking IP address. That means the person is smart.

But even smart people make mistakes, and this one will, too.

Hopefully, sooner rather than later.

I've just read through the final email, the one Starla received with the photo attached when my cell rings.

"Crawford."

"Sir, I think you should come to Starla's residence."

"What's going on? Is she okay?"

"She's not here, but we've had a car drive past about six times, always slowing down in front of the house. It looks like they're taking photos, but I can't make out if it's a man or a woman because the windows are tinted way past the legal limit."

"Pull them over for that," I suggest, reaching for my jacket as I shut my computer down.

"I'm in an unmarked," he reminds me, and I swear under my breath. "I do have a license plate number."

"And?"

"It comes back owned by a Theodora Fitzgerald of Bellevue. She's eighty-two. Which could explain the slowing down, if she's looking for a specific address."

"So you're alerting me over a lost grandma?" I demand.

"It looked suspicious to me, and you said to call in anything suspicious."

"If she comes back, let me know. I'm headed out of the office, but I'll be on my cell."

"Copy that."

He hangs up, and I walk out of the office. Just before I get to the door to the parking garage, I hear my name.

"Levi!"

I look back to see Matt Montgomery jogging toward me.

"Do you have a minute?"

"Sure, what's up?"

"We got the ME report on Francesca Smith."

"Are you telling me we weren't sure about the cause of death?"

"You're not funny," Matt says. "The ME found brain cancer, which I know doesn't really change anything now, but I thought it was interesting. Thought I'd pass the info along."

"Does he think the cancer is what made her crazy?"

Matt shrugs. "Who knows? I guess it could have. Maybe she was already a little *off*, and the cancer exacerbated the obsessive traits into a psychosis. It's definitely possible. But like I said, it doesn't change anything. Karen's still gone, along with the baby."

"Do you know how Jeremy's doing?"

Matt's face sobers more, and he doesn't look me in the eyes when he replies.

"He killed himself three days ago."

"Fuck." I stomp away and consider punching the wall, but it's cement, and I don't want to break my hand. "*Fuck.*"

"Yeah." Matt nods.

"And the kids?"

"They're with Karen's parents."

"At least he didn't kill them, too."

"Very true." Matt pats my shoulder. "There was nothing any of us could have done. Nothing."

"I hear you."

"But you don't believe me."

"Three people are dead, and I saw them all alive just days ago. I should have—"

"You did everything right. We're not God. You arrested her, and due to a flawed, human system, she hurt them anyway. It's tragic. It's horrifying, actually. But it's not your fault."

"Thanks." I nod once, then turn to leave the building. I have to switch gears from stalkers and death to my actual job of property theft.

This has been the weirdest month of my life.

I DROP THE stack of emails on the piano. Starla stops playing and stares at them and then looks up at me.

"Welcome home, dear."

"There are *hundreds* of emails there."

She looks at them again and then at me. "Okay."

"*Okay.*" I walk away from her, tug my jacket off, and throw it on the couch, then stomp into the kitchen for a bottle of water.

I wish it was scotch.

"Fifteen months," I begin after drinking half the bottle, "of emails. Not *six* months, Starla. Fifteen."

"I don't know what you want me to say. It *felt* like six months, but it's not like I have a timestamp on hand just in case someone asks me questions."

"I can live with that." I nod thoughtfully. "Time goes fast, and you've been busy. I get it. So you don't know how long ago they started. But the sheer number of them should have been a clue to tell someone."

"I just—"

"What? You just, what? Because I don't understand how this could happen. You have more money than I can wrap my head around, and a whole team of people whose only job is to *take care of you.* Yet you let this go on for fifteen damn months?"

"I'm just a human being." She stands and paces away. "I may be rich and famous, but I'm a *person.* Sometimes, people make mistakes, Levi."

I want to scream. I'm so damn frustrated with her, with Jeremy, with every damn thing today.

"My security team has enough to keep track of."

"Your security team is a joke and should have been fired *years* ago." I cross my arms over my chest.

"Oh, and you're perfect."

"Nope. Not even close. But I have a work ethic, and I would work circles around those clowns. You're an important person, Starla. Whether you want to admit it or not. And letting this go on for *months* is not okay."

"I get it." She holds up her hands in surrender. "I understand it's dangerous, and I've handed *everything* regarding my security to you. I'm cooperating. I don't know what else you want from me right now, Levi. Do you want to continue arguing? To shame me? To make me feel small? Because you're succeeding. I apologized. Now you're just beating the proverbial dead horse, and it's pissing me the fuck off."

I shove my hands through my hair, but before I can respond, she keeps talking.

"I wish I could take a day off from you."

Okay, that stings.

"And not because I'm trying to punish you, but because I need some *space*. I need a little time to cool off. To just *breathe*."

"You can have it."

Because, frankly, I need it too.

I reach for my phone and dial Jax's number.

"Who are you calling?"

I don't answer, I just hold her gaze as Jax picks up.

"Yello."

"Hey, it's Levi. Starla's going to come stay with you for a day or two. Cool?"

"Totally cool. Room's ready."

"She'll be there soon."

I hang up and look at the woman I love more than anything. Under normal circumstances, I could tell her that I'd see her tomorrow and just go home.

But now, someone wants to kill her, and that's not an option.

"Thanks for treating me like the child you, yourself, said you hated being treated as. It's awesome."

"I don't know what to fucking do," I say, holding my hands out to the sides. "We're pissed at each other, and I can't leave you alone, Starla. So pack a goddamn bag so I can take you to Jax and give you the space you want."

"I don't need a bag. Let's go."

She snatches her handbag from the table by the front door and marches ahead of me out to my car, sliding into the passenger seat. The air is thick with silent irritation as we drive the short distance to Jax and Logan's condo. Starla hops out of the car and hurries into the building without saying goodbye or even looking in my direction, and I don't get out to follow her.

I'm done with this godforsaken day.

I do pause to make sure the guys assigned to her are in place before I drive away. I want to go home, pour about six glasses of scotch, and go to bed. But that won't help anything, and if I'm alone, I'll just hate my own company.

So I drive to my parents' house. I promised a few weeks ago that I'd stop by and look at a leaky faucet.

I've been a little busy.

"Anyone here?" I ask as I walk inside my childhood home. The house has evolved over time with the addition of new furniture, different paint colors, and flooring. But the smell and the feelings it evokes when I walk inside will always be the same.

This is home.

"I'm in my office," Dad calls, so I wander to the room he keeps in the back of the house. Dad's mostly retired now, but he still likes to dabble at home. He's a successful financial planner, and I can see him doing this until the day he dies.

Numbers and music are his passion.

"What are you up to?" he asks as he pecks at his keyboard.

Dad never did learn to type.

"I had a couple of free hours, so I thought I'd drop by to fix that faucet Mom called me about a few weeks ago."

"That was four months ago," Dad says with a laugh. "We had a plumber come. It's fixed."

"Well, shit." I collapse into the chair facing him and rub my hand over my face. "I'm sorry, Dad. I guess time just slipped away from me."

Just the way it did for Starla and her emails.

God, I'm an ass.

"Not a big deal," he says and finishes what he was doing, then turns to look at me. "You don't look so hot."

"I don't feel so hot either." I smile ruefully. "Sometimes, you have a shitty day."

"If you're still breathing, it's a fantastic day." He winks and opens a cupboard, then pulls down two glasses and a bottle of scotch. "But a guy can always use a sip or two of this."

"You might have read my mind."

He slides a glass to me, and I take a sip.

"What's wrong?" he asks. "The job?"

"Yeah." I swallow the rest of the amber liquid and set the glass aside, then settle in to talk to my dad. I tell him the whole story. Because no one knows me better or gives better advice than Dad does.

fifteen

Starla

I feel like shit.

Worse than shit.

I feel like someone beat me over the head with a mallet, made me eat fourteen meals at a fast food joint, and left me for dead in the gutter.

"Ugh." I try to roll over, but my joints are sore, so it takes me a minute. By the time I'm settled on my other side, Jax barges through the door.

Okay, so he cracks it and quietly looks inside.

"Good morning, sunshine," he whispers.

I grunt a response, and he takes that as a *come on in*. So he does. He sits next to me and brushes my hair off my face.

"You look like shit."

"Yep."

"You didn't go to bed when you said you did."

I shrug a shoulder. "Nope."

"What did you do?"

"Wrote."

"I don't have a piano."

"Don't need one for lyrics." I yawn and frown at the dry mouth I feel. Jesus, you'd think I went on a four-day bender. "So sore. Headache."

"Because you haven't drunk any water in twenty-four hours, haven't eaten, and barely slept."

"Stop judging me."

I bury my face down in the pillow and regret my life choices.

"Come on, I'm going to take care of you before Levi discovers the state you're in and cuts off my balls."

"Levi's not the boss."

But I sit up and let Jax pull me from the bed to my feet. I am hungry. If I drank coffee, I'd have six cups.

Too bad it repulses me.

Must be left over from when I was a kid and my parents said caffeine was from Satan.

I follow Jax to the kitchen and sit at the island as he sets out to make me eggs and toast. He's a great cook.

Jax is actually good at most things.

"Should we talk about what's going on?" he asks as he cracks four eggs into a bowl.

"No. Because you'll yell at me, and I'm already pissed at myself enough."

"I won't yell."

"Yes, you will." I sigh and hunch over the counter, resting my pounding head in my hands. "It's not like I kept it a secret. I just didn't tell anyone."

"I don't even know what the hell is going on. You just suddenly have cops following you everywhere you go. It's a little unnerving."

"Trust me, I know." I fiddle with the salt and pepper shakers. "I've had some threatening letters and stuff. But I get a lot of weird mail. You know that. So, I just blew them off as another weirdo.

"But a few weeks ago, it escalated to the person sending photos as well, ones they Photoshopped to look like I'm dead."

He sets the bowl aside and leans on the counter, listening.

"I showed them to Levi, and he's doing the cop thing, investigating it all and trying to figure out who's sending them. So far, they can't tell who it is. But the letters are disturbing enough to want some protection at all times. That's why I can't ever be alone."

"I think we should invite the cops inside," Jax mutters, shaking his head. "How long?"

"I thought it was about six months, but the guy working on my electronics at Levi's office found emails that go back over a year."

"Holy shit, little girl."

"I know! See, I told you you'd yell at me. And trust me, I'm pissed at myself enough for both of us."

"Why didn't you ever say anything to anyone? More than a year ago, you were on tour and had a whole team of security with you at all times. All you had to do was hand it off to someone and tell them to deal with it."

"I know." I hang my head in my hands again. It's pounding the beat of a cha-cha. "I just don't remember them sounding threatening before. It's gotten way worse lately. And we're on it now. Levi will find him or her."

"You should call him."

"The stalker?"

"Levi."

"I think I'm still mad at him."

"Does he know you're not ghosting him again?"

I look up as he empties the eggs into the hot pan and starts to stir. "Of course, he does. I'm not ghosting him, for Christ's sake, I'm taking a breather."

"Maybe you should just call and tell him that. Just to put his mind at ease."

"Oh, for the love of Moses." I walk into the guest room and retrieve my phone. I haven't missed any calls or texts.

I dial Levi's number and frown when it goes to voicemail after only two rings.

"He sent me to voicemail."

"Wow, he's really mad at you."

My stomach rolls at the idea of Levi being so angry that he doesn't want to speak to me at all. I mean, I know that's how I was yesterday, but now in the light of a new day, I feel bad.

"Hi, Levi. It's Starla. Hey, I just wanted to touch base with you today and say I'm sorry for being a raging bitch, and I'm not trying to skip out on you or anything like that. I'm not really mad at you. I just need a day or two, but I'll be sure to text you and stuff, okay?" I bite my lip and wish I didn't sound so stupid. "I hope you have a good day. Okay. Bye."

When I hang up, Jax is staring at me like he's never met me before.

"What?"

"Jesus, you sound lovesick." He scoops some eggs onto a plate, adds two halves of toast, and passes the plate to me. "Just go find him."

"No. We've been together pretty much twenty-four-seven

for the past couple of weeks. A day apart won't kill us, and maybe I need it. He's amazing. But sometimes, he's intense."

I tell Jax about the day of the interview and how Levi fired the security guy.

"Well, it sounds like that guy was an idiot."

"Of course, he was an idiot, but that didn't give Levi the right to—"

"Okay, stop talking." Jax sets his fork down and leans in, looking all alpha and fierce. "When a man is trying his damn best to *protect* you from a real threat and love you at the same time, don't sit there and complain about it. Because let me tell you, there are plenty of men out there who wouldn't give a shit as long as you let them fuck you. If that's what you want, you can find it."

"That's not what I want."

"Then let him do his job, as both a cop and your man."

I frown down at my plate for a moment, thinking about Jax's words. "He hasn't ever said he loves me."

"I don't know why any of us do, because you're a stubborn ass," Jax says with a humorless laugh. "Of course, he loves you. He's done nothing but show you that he does, even if he hasn't said the words."

"Yeah." I scrub my hand over my face in frustration. "You're right. You're absolutely right. And I've done my best to cooperate with him. I'm *never* alone, Jax."

"And for you, that's like being at Guantanamo."

"Exactly. And yesterday, when Levi came home and immediately started accusing me of basically allowing someone to stalk me for a year, I just couldn't take it anymore. It's a *lot*. I wanted a day off from all of it."

"From the tone of his voice, it sounded like he did, too. He was frustrated when he called."

"You're right. Time apart isn't the death of a relationship."

"No, and I'm always happy to see you. I'm glad he called me."

"Me, too."

I take a bite of eggs, but they taste like cardboard. It's not Jax's fault. Everything is tasteless.

"You know what you need?"

"A lobotomy?"

"No, smartass. You need a girls' night out. And I'll even take one for the team and go with you, even though those girls are scary when they've had alcohol."

"There's no way I can go out dancing, Jax. It would be a security nightmare."

"So rent out a club for the night. It'll be a private party."

"I'll just give you my AmEx. Take my money and arrange it."

"Are you kidding me?"

"No. Knock yourself out."

"Holy shit, I just died and went to heaven."

"YOU FOUND THE cutest dress for tonight," Meredith says. It's mid-afternoon, and we've been out shopping. The reasons are two-fold.

One, shopping is the ultimate therapy.

And two, I wanted something flirty and sassy for girls' night out, which Jax has miraculously arranged for tonight.

Byron, the police officer, has been with us all day, following us from store to store, always no more than ten feet away.

I offered to buy him lunch, but he declined.

"Does Levi know where we are?" I ask him.

"Yes, ma'am."

I nod and turn back to Meredith. "It's weird, don't you think?"

"No. I think it's sweet, and it makes me feel better that he's here. Just in case. Jax told me everything, by the way."

"I figured he would. It's okay, everyone should know. The more eyes looking for something off, the better I suppose."

"I'm not even going to get into the whole you-should-have-told-me-months-ago thing."

"I would appreciate it if you didn't." A familiar face catches my eye as we walk through the mall. "Belinda? Belinda, is that you?"

Her head swivels toward me as if she didn't see me earlier, but I could swear she was just watching me.

"Starla?" Belinda says in surprise. "Oh my gosh, hi!"

"Hey there." I hug her tightly and then turn to Meredith. "Do you remember Belinda? She comes to every show."

"Of course, I do," Mer says with a smile. "It's nice to see you."

"You, too," Belinda says. She's a tall brunette with short hair and doesn't usually wear makeup. She's always been a superfan, coming to every show on the west coast, and one of my biggest supporters on social media.

"Gosh, I haven't seen you in a while," I say. "Are you living in Seattle now?"

"Yeah, I've been here for about six months or so. I came

for a job."

"Good for you. How is your daughter? Angie?"

"Angel," she corrects me.

"Of course, I'm sorry. How is she feeling?"

I met Belinda and her daughter Angel through the Make-A-Wish Foundation *years* ago when Angel was so sick with cancer. But she pulled through. The last I heard, she was doing great.

"Oh, she—" Belinda swallows hard. "She passed away a year ago in July."

"Belinda, I'm so sorry." I tug her to me for another hug. "I hadn't heard. I'm so, so sorry." I pull away. "Is there anything you need? Anything I can do?"

She shakes her head. "No, thanks. I'm fine. I'm going to be late for something, so I'd better go."

"I didn't mean to hold you up. Take care, Belinda."

She nods and hurries off, and I exchange a sad look with Meredith.

"That's so sad. I thought she was acting weird, but now I know why," Mer says, shaking her head. "I'd be acting weird too if I was in her shoes."

"It's horrible," I agree as we continue walking. I glance back at Byron, who's currently talking into his phone ten feet away. "Should we get some ice cream?"

"The answer to ice cream is always yes."

***

"YOU KNOW I'M not hot after your husband, right?"

Sam and I are sitting at a booth in the dark club. Most of the girls are on the dance floor, but some are at the bar. I asked

Sam to join me so I could clear the air. I've been thinking about this since my talk with Nat and Luke.

"Dude, if I thought you were after my husband, I wouldn't be here."

"Well, I figured that. I just wanted to make it perfectly clear to you that I respect and like you, and Leo is a lucky guy. I'm happy for both of you."

"Thank you," she says after sipping her margarita. "I didn't like you for a long time. I won't say I can't be jealous. But when you're married to someone like Leo Nash, jealousy would be the death of me. *Every*one wants a piece of him."

"Not me," I say adamantly. "And not just because I have a guy, but because that is ancient history."

"I'm not worried," she says with a confident smile. "I even like you. And trust me, I don't like just anyone."

I laugh in relief. "Well, good. And back at you. I guess being guarded is a necessity."

"Luke mentioned that you'd like to use the studio."

"If it's not being used for Nash stuff, I'd really love to. I'm in Seattle for at least a couple more months, and I've written some songs I'd like to record."

"I'll have Leo call you," she says.

"Thank you. Really."

She clinks her glass to mine just as Jules and Natalie come join us from the dance floor.

Brynna, Stacy, and Meredith are dancing with Jax. Joy and Lia are at the bar with Alecia. Anastasia, Lia's sister, is with the DJ, discussing what songs to play next.

They're a fun group of women. Actually, that's not right. They're a *ridiculously* fun group of women.

"God, I'm out of shape," Nat says as she takes a sip of her drink.

"You need to hit the gym more," Jules says as she tries to take a sip of her martini. But she misses the straw, and it stabs her in the cheek. "I'm such a lightweight these days. Two drinks and I'm under the table."

"Or *on* it," Nat says. "It's too bad Nic and Meg couldn't come."

"They have tiny babies at home," Jules says. "Nic and Matt's baby was *finally* born, and they just got home with her a few days ago."

"Awe, that's awesome." I sigh happily at the thought. Nic wanted kids for years but wasn't able to get pregnant because of being a diabetic and having PCOS. But they adopted a baby girl, and I just couldn't be happier for them.

"Let's send them a selfie of all of us," Jules says. "Come on, hold up your glasses."

We comply, smiling for Jules' phone as she snaps the photo and sends it to Nic and Meg.

"The waitress is bringing another round," Lia says as she and Joy join us. This is a club full of dozens of tables, and we're all crammed around this one.

I love it.

"Are you sure you don't want anything stronger than Coke?" Joy asks me.

"No, I don't drink much alcohol."

"More for us," Lia says with a smile. "Also, your makeup is *on point* tonight."

"Thanks. Jax did it."

"Those women are crazy," Jax says as he hurries to the

booth and scoots in next to me. "All of you are fucking nuts."

"Speak of the devil." I smile at my friend. "Why are you afraid of women?"

"I'm not. Unless it's the Montgomery clan, and then it's fucking frightening. You all dance up on me and ask me to describe a blowjob from a man's point of view and all of the other shit. This is why I don't come to girls' night out."

"You love us," Mer reminds him. Stacy and Brynna are behind her, laughing with their arms around each other. "Let's pull another table over. Make it a big one."

"Good idea," Brynna says, and in no time at all, there's enough table space and seats for everyone. The DJ has lowered the music just a smidge so we can hear each other, and a fresh wave of drinks is delivered.

"I'm just shocked y'all wanted to come out on a Wednesday," I confess. "It's a school night for all of you."

"Not for me," Sam says with a laugh.

"Luke's awesome about stuff like this," Nat says with a flick of her wrist, narrowly avoiding knocking over her drink.

"Honestly, all of our husbands are," Brynna says with a smile. "And let's be frank, they'll all get a blowjob of the century for tonight. Not that we shouldn't be able to go out with our friends, but it's pretty cool."

"Let's talk about blowjobs," Stacy says, eyeing Jax, who sinks down in his seat.

"No," Jax says.

"Don't be a killjoy," Anastasia says. "Not all of us have heard this, so you need to spill it."

"I've talked about it, over and over."

"Not when we were here," Joy reminds him. "Come on,

you like being the center of attention."

"What do you want to know?"

Of course, they wore him down. Joy was right, Jax *does* like being the center of attention.

"What does it feel like?" Lia asks.

"It feels like a blowjob."

"Well, we don't have dicks," Anastasia reminds him. "So, explain please."

"It feels like someone is sucking on your skin, and it feels really good."

"That's it?" Brynna asks. "That's not what you said last time."

"I'm going to write a fucking manual and just hand it out at the beginning of GNO so you can reference it and I don't have to go over it again."

We laugh at him, and he proceeds to describe a blowjob from start to finish.

"Orgasms!" Natalie exclaims, her glass in the air. "That's what I'm talkin' about."

"You've had exactly *one* drink," Jules says to her. "How are you already slurring your words?"

"I don't drink much these days. I have a hundred kids now."

"Trust me, I know. I was there when you had them. I'm sick of looking at your vajayjay," Jules says. "Stop making me look at it."

"I'm done having kids," Nat says. "No more vajayjay."

"Thank the baby Jesus," Jules replies. "Nate thinks he wants more, but I can't make another one stick, so we're done."

"What do you mean?" I ask her.

"He wants more kids."

"No." I giggle, enjoying these women very much. "About the making it stick."

"I've had a couple miscarriages," Jules says, the smile slipping from her face. "And I don't want to do that anymore. It's sad. We have Stella, and she's perfect and wonderful, and it's okay for her to be an only child."

"She's not," Nat reminds her. "We have billions of kids in this family. She's not growing up alone."

"Exactly." Jules drains the last of her drink. "And Nate's come around. He really didn't want me to come out tonight. He totally pouted."

She lowers her brows, tucks in her chin, and starts speaking in a low voice, mimicking her husband.

"Julianne, if you think you're going out tonight, you can think again. I'll tie you to my bed."

She keeps talking, making us all laugh so hard, I'm pretty sure I pee my pants a little.

"I will spank your ass, Julianne."

A tall figure walks through the club and stands behind Jules. We're all snickering, and I know someone should tell her, but it's so damn *funny*.

"If you don't do what I say, I'll bend you over this counter and show you who's boss."

"You'd better be talking about me, Julianne."

Her eyes widen. She stares at me across the table.

"He's behind me, isn't he?"

"Yes, he is," Nate replies. "I came to get you."

"We live around the block," she says with a frown. "I walked, remember?"

"And if you think I'm letting you walk home alone at this

time of night, you're crazy."

She lowers her brows and tucks in her chin.

"If you think I'm letting you walk home alone, blah blah blah."

We dissolve into a fit of giggles, and Nate's lips twitch with humor, but he doesn't laugh. I don't know if I've ever seen him laugh.

"Where's Stella?" Jules asks him.

"With Mrs. Pierce."

"You gotta love grandmotherly neighbors," Jules says. "You all need to get one."

"Are you ready?" Nate asks her.

"I guess I am now." She sighs and stands. "It is a school night, after all."

"It's two in the damn morning," Nate says, surprising us all.

"Wait, it is?" I ask, and we all check our phones.

"Aww, look!" Jules turns her phone to show us. "Nic and Meg both sent photos back, toasting us with baby bottles."

"So cute," Lia says. "I guess they'll be kicking us all out of here."

"Thank God," Jax grumbles, but I bump him with my shoulder.

"You love this."

"Yeah. It's fun."

Just as we're gathering our things and getting ready to go, another man walks across the dance floor, straight to me.

"Levi."

"We're done."

My heart stops. "What?"

"We're done being apart. You've had eighteen hours, and

that's about sixteen too many for me. I'm taking you home with me."

I take a deep breath. The DJ turns the music up, playing one of my favorite slow songs.

"Dance with me first," I say, tugging him out to the floor.

"One dance." He pulls me into his arms, and we sway back and forth while everyone watches. "And then I'm taking you home."

"Deal."

sixteen

Starla

"**I** swear, it's been one thing after another with this place," Natalie says the next day. We're all at the house, and the hot water system has gone out.

"Things happen," Luke says calmly and makes a phone call, stepping away for the conversation.

"He'll just call his assistant, and it'll get taken care of," Nat says.

"You probably didn't have to come over," Levi says. "I could have told him this was the case."

"Well, we're landlords, so we should come and check it out." Natalie smiles. "And it's always good to see you both. Even though we just saw you last night."

"Or this morning." I take a long drink of water. I didn't drink any alcohol last night, and I still feel dehydrated. But, man, we had a blast.

Luke returns to the room. "My assistant is on it. As soon as we have someone scheduled to come and fix it, I'll let you know."

"That's great, thanks," I reply just as my phone pings with a message. "Sorry, guys, I'm waiting for an email. I have to check this really quick."

"No worries," Nat says as I open my email, and it's like deja vu, all over again.

God, you're so fucking smug.

You don't care. At all. You just don't care. And that might be the worst thing of all. The worst transgression. Your indifference is going to cost you your life.

I can't keep reading, and I don't even check to see if there's a photo.

"I can't fucking believe it. This is a *brand new* email address!"

"Give it to me."

I pass the phone to Levi.

"I'm supposed to be here on vacation, and I'm as stressed now as I ever was. It's absolutely ridiculous. I'm *done.*" I'm so damn pissed, there's a red haze covering everything. "I'm done with this whole fucked-up situation. I need to just go away where no one can find me."

"We'll go anywhere you want," Levi says with a calm voice. He's tapping the screen of my phone, and when he looks up at me, his brown eyes are compassionate and furious. "Anywhere."

"I have a suggestion," Natalie says. "We found a little town in Montana called Cunningham Falls. It's beautiful and private. If you trust me, I can arrange everything. Nothing will be in either of your names, and you can just relax."

I look at Levi.

"It's totally up to you," he says.

"I'm in," I reply. "Thank you so much."

"Oh, it's my pleasure." Natalie waves me off. "Let me make

some calls. Go ahead and pack a bag because we should have you out of here by this afternoon."

"So soon?"

"Hell, yes, we'll get you out of here and relaxing in no time." Luke smiles and starts making calls. "Hey, Christian, I need your plane . . ."

c∾

TRUE TO THEIR word, Luke and Nat arranged for us to leave in less than three hours.

On a private jet.

Bound for Montana.

"Have you ever been to Montana?" Levi asks. The pilot just told us we're about twenty minutes from landing.

"I think I did a couple concerts in Montana back in the day, but I was never there long enough to really know what city I was in. You?"

"Nope," he replies with a grin. "It'll be a new adventure for both of us."

"It's kind of exciting. I can't believe they sent a private jet for us."

"That's what you do for people you love, Starla. You help them."

I can't look Levi in the eyes. I don't know how comfortable I am with the *L* word yet.

"It was still nice of them."

We're circling around a little town below. The mountains we flew over to get here are gorgeous.

It feels like we're in a different country.

The plane makes a smooth landing and taxis away from the main terminal toward an area with private planes of all sizes.

Once we're stopped, the door is opened, and we climb out to find an SUV parked nearby with a couple standing next to it.

"Hey there, I'm Jenna Hull."

A beautiful blond woman approaches us with a smile.

"Natalie said you'd meet us here," Levi says. "Thank you."

"Absolutely." She shakes both of our hands and then turns to the man. "This is my husband—"

"You're Christian Wolfe." My mouth is open. I probably look like a crazy fan-girl.

I can't help it. Christian Wolfe is my favorite actor *ever.* He can sing and dance, and I've secretly longed to work with him for as long as I can remember. He's so damn sexy, it should be illegal.

Of course, I would never say that in front of Levi.

"Guilty," Christian says with a smile. "And you're Starla."

"I'm surprised you two have never met before," Jenna says.

"I think we've been at the same parties after awards shows, but no. We've never met." Christian watches me with concerned blue eyes. "You okay?"

"I'm going to be great, thanks. And it's a pleasure to meet you. I didn't realize you and your wife were our hosts. I guess I didn't connect the dots, but now I realize you were in a Luke Williams' film last year."

"And doing another one next year," Christian confirms. "Come on, let's get you guys settled."

We climb into the back of the SUV, and Christian drives us away from the airport toward a big mountain.

"So, this is Cunningham Falls," Jenna says. "It's a small

town, but we do get a lot of tourists in the summer and winter because of all the outdoor activities. It's pretty calm right now thanks to it being the off-season."

"I'll need to be in touch with local law enforcement," Levi says.

"That's my brother, Brad. He's the chief of police," Jenna replies. "I'll give you his number."

"Perfect."

We drive through a town that's something out of a Hallmark movie. The downtown area is cute with plenty of shops and restaurants. The backdrop of the mountain is picturesque.

"This is beautiful." My face is practically pressed to the window. "Didn't Joslyn Meyers grow up here?"

Joslyn is another famous pop singer. She's quite a bit younger than me, but she's incredibly talented, and although I've only met her a couple of times, she seems nice.

"She did," Jenna says. "We've had quite a few people go on to be famous. And we get our share of celebrities who come here for vacation. Some buy homes here."

"Really. I'm intrigued. Don't you have paparazzi issues?" I ask.

"Not really," Christian says. "It's one of the reasons I love it so much. The locals are used to seeing celebrities and rarely make a fuss. It's been refreshing, to say the least."

"Nice."

Once he's driven through town, Christian turns onto a windy road that leads up the mountain.

"This is Whitetail Mountain," Jenna informs us. "It's a world-class ski resort. But again, it's quiet this time of year. Most of the tourists are gone. I don't have any other guests this week, so you'll have plenty of privacy."

"This is incredibly generous," I reply.

"We like Luke and Nat a lot, so when they said they had a friend who needed anonymity and relaxation, we were happy to help," Christian says.

We drive past a small village. There are ski lifts that are currently not moving.

"They run the lifts on the weekends," Jenna says as if she can read my mind. "I recommend going up to have a look around. The view is crazy beautiful."

Levi takes my hand in his, links our fingers, and gives me a squeeze. I never thought I'd like a man so physically affectionate.

But I do. I so do.

"Here it is," Christian says, and I feel my jaw drop for the second time today.

Ahead of us are three treehouses. They're at least thirty feet in the air, and they sit right next to one of the chairlifts.

The one on the far left is bigger than the others, but aside from size, they all look exactly the same.

"Whoa," Levi says.

"Wait until you see inside of them," Jenna replies as we all climb out of the SUV.

Levi and Christian grab our bags, and Jenna leads us into the biggest of the three units.

"I've stocked the kitchen with plenty of staples, but there are two grocery stores in town if you need anything else. Unfortunately, all of the stores are closed up here on the mountain for the off-season.

"The Wi-Fi information, along with a list of restaurants and other things to do in the area is in this book." She lifts a binder on the kitchen counter for us to see and then leads us through the living room to the deck beyond. "This door is heavy."

"Whoa," Levi says again when we step outside. The deck is spacious, big enough to hold at least twenty people. There's an outdoor eating space and a fantastic view of the entire ski resort.

"You'll have to come out here at night," Christian says. "The stars are amazing here."

"I can't wait."

"Come on," Jenna says, leading us back inside. "There's more to see."

She's not kidding. Downstairs, there are more bedrooms and bathrooms, and another deck with a private hot tub. The main floor has the kitchen and living space, and a large master bedroom and bathroom.

"Now, the top floor," she says with a grin. "This is my favorite."

I can see why. There are more beds up here, and a ladder leading to a turret.

"Watch," Christian says as Jenna flips a switch and the ceiling of the turret lights up with hundreds of tiny twinkle lights, making it look like a night sky.

"I'll be writing songs up here," I whisper as Levi hugs me from behind. "This is beautiful. Thank you again."

"Our pleasure," Jenna says. "How do you feel about a trip to the spa tomorrow?"

"I am a sucker for the spa."

"It's a date, then."

Once Jenna and Christian say their goodbyes and leave, Levi and I stand in the kitchen, just staring at each other.

"Did the past five hours happen?" I ask, feeling shell-shocked.

"Seems so." He crosses to me and pulls me in for a long, tight hug. "What do you want to do first?"

"Sleep. I didn't sleep well without you."

He kisses my forehead.

"Let's sleep, then."

⌒

"THIS IS INCREDIBLE."

We're lying on the mattress in the turret. All the lights are off, including the twinkle lights, and it's late, well past sunset. The sky through the big windows is clear and *alive* with so many stars, it would be impossible to count them all.

"Did you see that?" Levi asks, pointing.

"Yeah, that's the third shooting star I've seen."

"Did you make a wish?"

I turn to look at his handsome face in the moonlight. "Am I supposed to wish on shooting stars?"

"Well, sure. It's a thing."

He looks at me and leans over to brush the tip of his nose against mine.

"Didn't you know that?"

"Never heard of it. But there are still a lot of things I've never heard of." I shrug and look up again, transfixed by the night sky.

"How did you learn?" he asks. "After you left and made it to LA, you would have been unaware of not just academic things, but pop culture of all kinds."

"I was a sponge," I admit. "I watched TV constantly. Read magazines. I couldn't get enough of the radio, listening to everything I could get my ears on.

"After Donald took me on, he sent me to a tutor, five days a week, until I had the basics under my belt. I read fine, and I can do basic math, plus I learned a lot about history. I didn't even know who the president was when I met Donald. So I pay attention, and I soak it all in."

Levi rolls to his side, bracing his head on his hand, looking down at me.

"You're smart, Starla."

"Yeah." I drag my fingertip down the length of his nose. "I am. If I wasn't, I would still be there."

"I'm glad you're not."

My finger lands on his lips, and he kisses it sweetly.

"Me, too. Okay, enough of the depressing stuff. I need an *L* word."

He raises an eyebrow, and I look back up through the window.

"Why?"

"I'm writing a song, and I want an *L* word in this spot."

"How does it go?"

I clear my throat. I'm so damn nervous. Why I thought this was a good idea, I'll never know.

But here we are, and I already opened my big mouth, so there's no going back now.

With my eyes pinned to the stars above, I start to sing.

There's a star
In the sky
Close my eyes
This wish is mine

Through all the pain
All the tears
Loneliness
And worthless fears

He would find me
He would see me
And through my faults
He would still . . .

I stop singing, and suddenly, Levi is over me, cradling my head in his arms and kissing me like his very life depends on it.

"He does love you." His voice is hoarse with emotion. The moonlight shines in his eyes. "Is that the *L* word you were looking for, sweetheart?"

I nod and bite my lip, watching him through tear-filled eyes. I didn't know how badly I needed to hear the words until now.

"Loving you is the easiest thing I've ever done."

"I'm not easy." I laugh softly.

"Loving you is," he insists, brushing his thumbs over the apples of my cheeks. "Even when I want to yell in frustration, I love you so much, I ache with it."

He kisses my nose and down to my lips again. We're already naked, having come up to the turret after a vigorous round of sex down in the master bedroom after we woke from our long nap.

He nudges his way between my legs and sinks inside me easily. Fully. Making me sigh in happiness.

He takes my hands, links our fingers, and presses them over my head as he makes slow, sweet love to me, kissing my neck and moving in long, delicious motions, sliding his lean body over mine as if we were made to fit together, just like this.

Every time with Levi is extraordinary.

This time with him is *everything*.

I lift my legs higher up on his sides, and he sinks even deeper.

"You amaze me," he whispers against my skin. "You're so fucking beautiful, I can't stand it. I never stop wanting you."

His hands slide down my arms, but I keep them above my head. He slips one hand under my ass, tipping me up just a bit and making the angle *incredible*.

"Holy hell."

"You *are* love for me, Starla. You're the most important part of my life."

I cradle his face in my hands.

"I love you, too, Levi Crawford."

His eyes close as if he's so relieved he can't help himself. And with the quiet night around us, we let go.

seventeen

Levi

"Where is she now?"

I'm in Brad Hull's office in the heart of Cunningham Falls. It's nothing special. It's certainly not as palatial as the chief of Seattle PD's is.

But something tells me Brad does more than ride a desk here in Montana.

"She's at the spa with your sister. I don't believe anyone knows where we are, or that we were followed, but out of courtesy and for my own peace of mind, I wanted to give you a heads-up. And, of course, let you know I'm here and tell you that I'm carrying a weapon."

"I appreciate that. Although almost everyone carries a weapon at some time or another around here." Brad leans back in his chair, frowning. "It's odd to me that the stalker has been able to mask their IP so well."

"Same here. We have some of the best IT people on the west coast working on it, and so far, they've come up empty-handed."

"Well, I hope you find this asshole soon. In the meantime,

I'll have my guys keep an eye out for anything out of the ordinary. Things like that are easier to see in a small town like this."

"I hadn't thought of that." I rub my cheek in thought. "But it makes perfect sense. Thank you."

"Anytime. Are you guys up at the treehouses?"

"Yes, and they're incredible."

He smiles proudly. "Jenna's done a great job up there. Enjoy yourselves while you're here, and if you need anything at all, we're a phone call away."

"I have it." I raise my phone and give it a little wag. After I shake his hand, I walk out of the police station to the SUV that Christian loaned us rather than have to rent a car in our name.

Between Luke, Christian, and myself, we thought of everything to keep Starla and I completely untraceable. To anyone looking for us, it would appear that we simply disappeared.

I like it. But I'm still careful because Starla's life is on the line, and I will *not* fuck this up.

I glance at the time. Starla and Jenna will be at the spa for at least another hour, so I drive around town, soaking it in.

It's small but well-kept. The downtown has a rustic, woodsy atmosphere without sending it to over-the-top cheesy. There are restaurants, dress shops, a flower shop, and finally, toward the end of the main street, a coffee shop.

I find a parking space out front and walk inside Drips & Sips, in desperate need of caffeine. It's bigger than it looks outside, with a nice gift shop and seating in the back.

"What can I get you?"

"Coffee. Highly caffeinated."

"We have plenty of that." The barista smiles as she taps the screen of her computer. "Where are you visiting from?"

"How do you know I'm visiting?"

She laughs now as she hands me my change and turns to the espresso machine to make my drink.

"Because I know everyone in this town, and I ain't ever seen you around here before."

"Guilty. I'm from California."

She nods and continues to talk about tourists and some of the things I should go see while I'm here, but I ignore her, keeping an eye on the shop, making mental notes of who and what I see.

It's a habit of the job.

A redheaded woman sits at a table in the back with headphones on, typing vigorously on a laptop. An older grey-haired woman drinks coffee with a younger friend, both deep in conversation.

The bell above the door rings as a tall man in a suit walks in, waves at the barista, then walks quickly to where the redhead is typing.

"Ty!" the woman exclaims and stands to hug him.

"Here you go. Have a fun vacation."

"Thanks." I wave and walk back out to the car, ready to go and find my girl and take her back to the treehouse.

"I GET IT," Starla says a couple of days later. We're standing at the top of Whitetail Mountain after riding the chairlift all the way up. There's a place up here to buy a beer or a meal, but aside from that, we're surrounded by trees and more mountains.

"What do you get?" I ask as I watch Starla stare out across

the valley before us.

"Why people want to live here." She smiles over at me. "It's quiet. The people are *so nice*. And good-looking. Did you notice that?"

"No," I say with a laugh. "I don't think I was paying attention to that."

"It's almost weird," she says. "Anyway, I like it here."

"It's nice."

"But you don't want to live here."

"I'm a city boy," I confess with a shrug. "So, yes, this is beautiful, and I would definitely visit again, but I like living in Seattle."

"I get it." She walks over to the other side of the mountain, looking into Glacier National Park and toward Canada. "I guess I'm just enjoying the peacefulness of it."

"As you should. This is your vacation."

I take her hand in mine and pull it to my mouth, casually kissing her knuckles.

"Let's take the chair back down," she says, leading me to the chairlift. "The view is going to be off the hook."

"Let's do it."

There's no line when we arrive. The kid running the lift gives us instructions on where to stand, and we hop onto the chair, get settled, and he lowers the bar over us, securing us.

"I knew it," she says with a wide grin as we glide over the top of the mountain and see the valley below. There's a huge lake at the edge of the town, and we can see a dozen or so boats zooming over the water. "Today would be a *great* day to be on the water."

"Do you like to boat?"

"I don't know," she says. "I've never done it."

"Never?"

"I've been a little busy touring." She shrugs a shoulder and then points to the horizon. "Look! There's another town and lake way out there. Geez, we must be able to see fifty miles away."

She's like a kid, seeing the most amazing thing of her life. Her excitement is so palpable. She's been all over the world on tour, but it occurs to me that she would have always been in a hotel and a venue, not out exploring the sights.

We need to change that for her in the future.

"The spa was amazing the other day," she says as she swings her feet in the air. "I've been to some of the best spas in the world, and this one could go up against any of them any day of the week."

"That's quite an endorsement."

"It's the truth. I loved it."

I'm not watching the scenery, as gorgeous as it is. I'm watching Starla. She's come alive in the past three days since we've been here. She's relaxed and happy. And sexy as hell—but that's always the case.

I love seeing her like this, and if Cunningham Falls, Montana, does this for her, I'll buy her a vacation house here myself.

"I wonder if Donald is freaking out yet," she says, biting her lip.

"You didn't tell him where we were going?"

"I left my phone in Seattle," she confesses, and I realize I haven't seen her pull her phone out once. "I just wanted to disengage."

"Well, you've done a good job of it. Do you want me to call

Donald and let him know you're safe?"

"No." She sighs and watches as we approach the bottom of the lift. "He'll be fine. I'll call him when we get back in a couple days."

"WE RODE THE chairlift yesterday like you suggested," Starla tells Jenna as she eats some of the best garlic bread I've ever had. "It was *amazing*."

"I'm so glad you went," Jenna says. "I think they close the lift for the season next weekend, so it was good timing. And it was such a clear day yesterday, I bet you could see all the way to Canada."

"I can't believe how beautiful it is here," Starla says. "It doesn't look real."

"It's real." Christian grins. "I'm glad you've been enjoying the area."

"No one's recognized me," Starla says with awe. "And if they did, they didn't say a word. I went into a dress shop yesterday. What's it called?" She looks at me, but I can't remember.

"Dress It Up?" Jenna asks.

"Yes! Such cute things in there. I think I bought everything."

"Willa's married to my brother, Max," Jenna says. "Her store is fantastic."

"We'll definitely be back," Starla says with confidence, and Christian smiles at me.

"You haven't said a word."

"If the lady wants to come here on vacation, her wish is my command."

"Do you like it here?" Jenna asks me, and all three pairs of eyes turn to me.

"I do. It's a great little town. Like I told Starla yesterday, I'm a city boy. I love Seattle, and I'll always want to live there. But this is a great place to visit."

"I hope you'll visit often," Jenna says with a smile. "Now, we have to figure out what to order for dinner before the waitress gets mad. Ciao has the best pasta in town, but they also have amazing pizza."

"I'm going to have to hike that mountain tomorrow rather than ride the chair. My ass is going to grow ten sizes after I eat all this pasta."

"So worth it," Jenna says. "So, so worth it."

"OH MY GOD."

My fingers tangle in Starla's hair as I surface from a deep sleep. She's sucking me off, that magical mouth of hers working me over like nothing else I've ever experienced.

I don't know what I did to deserve this, but I'd gladly do it every single day for the rest of my life.

She cups my balls and rubs that skin just behind them firmly, and I come up off the bed.

"Christ."

She grins but doesn't stop.

"If you don't want me to come in your mouth, stop now."

But she doesn't stop, and that alone makes me want to lose it. She's moving faster, jerking me harder, and I can't hold it together.

I can't stop the orgasm moving through me like a fucking freight train.

I'm still heaving, lying on my back, staring at the ceiling when she climbs over me and smiles down at me.

"Good morning, handsome."

"Holy hell."

"I'll be right back."

She hurries off the bed and runs into the bathroom. I hear the water running for what seems like a long time, and then she scurries back.

I smell toothpaste on her breath.

"Good morning." I find my voice.

"That was fun."

"That was a fucking blast."

She giggles and tucks herself against my side, snuggling in deep. She draws circles on my chest, through the light spattering of hair there.

"Couldn't sleep?" I ask.

"It's almost ten."

I frown and reach for my phone. Sure enough, it's 9:45. "I never sleep this late."

"You're finally relaxing."

She's right. I don't think I've been this relaxed since I started my job on the force twenty years ago. I definitely haven't slept this hard, or this late, that's for sure.

"Maybe Montana is better for you than you're willing to admit," she says.

"Do *you* want to make a home here?" I ask her, rolling onto my side so I can look her in the eyes.

"I don't know." She frowns slightly, thinking it over. "To be honest, I don't think I've ever felt like I had a home base. What I grew up in was a prison. I've been touring for *so long*. The bus was home, and then the plane. I have a mausoleum in LA."

"A what?"

"The place is *huge*. And it echoes, and it's perfect for photo shoots. I mean, yes, the closet is to die for, and I like pretty things so I'll always need a huge closet, but the house is twelve thousand square feet, Levi."

"Wow."

"Yeah. I could get lost in it. There are rooms I've *never* been in. It used to be one of the Kardashians' houses. I forget who.

"Anyway, it's way too big for me, and it's not my home. If it was, I would have stayed there during my mandatory ninety days off."

"That's true."

"I'd say the people in Seattle are my home." Her voice quiets to a whisper at the last word. "Meredith and her family, Jax and Logan, and now you."

I tip up her chin so I can kiss her soft lips.

"How long are you going to be a police officer?"

"That's an interesting question."

She sighs. "I know. I'm curious."

"The plan has been to be with the force until I retire."

"So, more than twenty more years?" She frowns. "That's a long time."

"Most cops don't work the field that long. They move up and work a desk, delegating to those in the field. I've thought of doing that, too. When I'm a little older."

"What you do is dangerous."

"Sometimes."

She chews her lip.

"Are you worried about me, sweetheart?"

"Of course, I am." She frowns and cups my cheek. "I love you. If something were to happen, it would destroy me."

"Nothing's going to happen."

"Don't say that." She covers my lips with her finger. "You can't promise me that. I've heard it before and still lost. We don't know what will happen. And I'm not asking you to leave the force, because it's who you are, and you're good at it. Amazing. It's your passion. If you asked me to give up music, we wouldn't be together."

"I don't hear you asking me to quit. You're worried."

"Yeah."

"I think we should table this discussion for now because we're on vacation, and we should be laughing and having lots of sex."

Her frown turns into a smirk.

"When do we have to go back?"

"We can go anytime," I reply.

"Let's stay here, in the treehouse, one more day."

My hand glides down her side to her hip.

"Okay, but there will be rules."

"Really? What kind of rules?"

"Well, for starters, no clothes are allowed. This is the nudity day of the vacation."

She laughs, her whole body shaking with delight. "Ooh, I like nudity day. What else?"

"We don't leave this bed unless it's for sustenance. We have bread and peanut butter in the kitchen. We won't starve."

"Delicious." She kisses my chin and slides her hand over my

ass. "Have I told you how much I like your butt?"

"I don't think you have."

"I seriously like your butt." She kisses my neck. "It's firm and just the right size."

"I'm glad you approve."

"Do you have any other rules?"

"We'll make them up as we go."

eighteen

Starla

"Again," Leo Nash, international rock god, instructs me from behind the piano. We're in the booth, and we're running through the song, making it perfect before we record it. "You keep missing the note in the second verse."

"You know, I wrote this song," I remind him. "Maybe that's how it's supposed to sound."

"Is it?"

"No." I laugh and smile at Sam when she comes into the room with two bottles of water. "Your husband is a slave driver."

"Don't let him bully you," Sam says before planting a kiss on his head. "Need anything else? I'm going to head over to Mom and Dad's for a bit."

"No, thanks, Sunshine," Leo says before pulling her into his lap to kiss the hell out of her. "Tell them I said hi."

"Tell them yourself. You're coming to dinner at six. Don't forget."

"Yes, ma'am."

She winks at him, sends me a wave, and is out the door again.

"I like her," I say, shifting the paper on the music stand. "A lot."

"Me, too."

"Was it hard? Settling down? What with the job we have and all?"

He drinks his water, thinking about it. "Marrying Sam, being with her, was the easiest thing I've ever done. My life doesn't work without her. But it's not been easy finding the balance. I tour constantly. Or, did."

"Did?"

"Yeah, we're slowing it down some. We'll still tour, but for shorter stretches, and we'll go longer in between. I'm at a place where I want to make music, but I also want to be home more."

"Yeah." I sigh and sit on the stool, looking at the floor.

"Is this about Levi?"

"Yeah," I say again. "I just don't see how people like us can make it work, you know? I'll be gone soon. I only come to Seattle about once a year to see the family, and that's usually around a tour date. Levi's a cop, and I would never ask him to give that up."

"Maybe you wouldn't have to ask him," Leo suggests.

"Well, he isn't volunteering either. And I don't blame him. Maybe I'm just overthinking it all."

"How much longer are you in Seattle?"

"Another month. And then it's back in the studio and to the rest of the grind."

"You sound thrilled."

I laugh and shrug. "I love it, too, you know? I love the

lifestyle. But it's exhausting."

"Balance," Leo says as if it should be the easiest thing in the world.

"I haven't had anyone in my life that I was afraid to lose. Not for a long time," I confess. "But I'm terrified now. Levi understands me. He reads me well. He's a rock star at putting up with my moods."

"Moods are what artists do best," Leo says.

"He takes care of me, you know? Not financially or anything, because . . . duh. But he takes care of my soul. My heart. In ways I didn't know I needed."

"You're in love with him."

"So much it makes me lose my breath."

"Good for you, my friend." He smiles, but when I don't smile in return, he sobers. "What is it?"

"I don't come from love, Leo. What I knew my whole life was dark and mean and just . . . *bad*."

"I understand. I come from all of that, as well."

My gaze flies to his. "You do?"

"Oh, yeah. The foster system isn't a walk in the park."

I swallow hard and feel tears threaten. He might be one of the few people I've ever met who could possibly understand me.

"I'm afraid to love Levi because . . . what if I don't know how?"

"Man." He exhales loudly. "He fell in love with you because you showed him who *you* are. He loves you because of the way you love him in return, Starla. And, frankly, it might sound trite, but you have to talk to him. You have to confide in him about your fears because they'll fester. Hell, Sam and I have been together since Jesus was born, and we still have our moments. Talk to him. And despite where you come from, you *know* how to love. Hell, a person doesn't write a song like *Wish* and not know love."

I grin, thinking about the song we're working on. It's the one from that night in the turret in Montana.

When we confessed our love.

"Now, enough of all of this crap about feelings. Let's record a song."

I roll my eyes. "You're such a man."

"Thank you for noticing."

The next hour goes so much better. I'm able to hit the note in the second verse, and by the time we've recorded the song, I'm absolutely in love with it.

"This is damn good," Leo says proudly. "It's going to be a big hit for you. Feel free to record in my studio anytime."

"Don't make an offer like that unless you mean it, because I have a feeling I'll be spending a lot more time in Seattle."

"I do mean it. The next time I have all the guys here, you should come jam with us."

"I'd like that. Thanks."

"You're welcome. And, Starla?"

"Yeah?"

"You deserve Levi and all the happiness he brings to you. You can have both the man and the job. You'll figure it out."

I nod and pat him on the shoulder. I don't pull away when he tugs me in for a hug.

"Thanks. You're right, we'll figure it out."

Once I'm in my little Jag and headed toward Seattle, I call Levi.

"What are you wearing?" I ask when he picks up.

"Way more than I'd like to be."

"No, if you're in public, you should be fully dressed. I don't share."

He chuckles in my ear. "What are you up to? How's the recording going?"

"We're done, and it was fabulous. I'll play it for you when you get home. I'm headed there now. Should we do salads from Salty's tonight?"

"I don't want you to be home alone," he says. "The guys had to be pulled off your detail for another investigation, and I don't have anyone else on it yet."

"Levi, I'm fine. I'm going right home, where I'll lock the door and set the alarm. And you'll be home in like two hours. Seriously, it's okay."

"Don't forget to set the alarm." His voice is hard. He's in bossy-cop mode.

It's kind of hot.

"Ten-four, good buddy."

"You're in a good mood."

"I know, I had a good afternoon with Leo, the song is fantastic, and he gave me some sage advice."

"What's that?"

"To basically keep doing what I'm doing."

"Well, okay then. I'm glad it went well, and I can't wait to hear the song. I think I can get things wrapped up here in just a little bit, and then I'll be there."

"You don't have to rush."

"Yes. I do. Love you, babe. See you soon."

"Love you back."

I click off, and before the radio has a chance to come through the speakers, my phone rings.

It's my assistant, Rachel.

"Holy shit, I haven't talked to you in *years.*"

She laughs, the sound a welcome one after not hearing from her in so long.

"I know. You went on vacation and left me to my own devices. So I went on my own little vacation, but I thought it was time to check in on you. How are you feeling?"

"Much better than the last time you saw me."

"That's awesome. I'm glad to hear it. I'm actually in Seattle for a few days and thought it would be fun to have dinner."

"What? When did you get here? Why don't I know this?"

"Calm down, woman. I just got here this morning. So, we're on for dinner then?"

"Absolutely. Does six work?"

"Six is perfect. Just text me where to meet you. I'm excited to see you."

"Me, too. Yay! Okay, see you later."

"Bye."

Today is a really good day. I was beginning to worry about Rachel. It's not unusual for her to go off and do her own thing when we're between tours or if I don't need her. But I start to miss her because we spend *so much* time together when we are traveling and working. She's my right hand. I don't know what I would do without her.

Traffic is light for this time of day, which is a miracle in itself. The rain that pounded down just a few hours ago has cleared, and it looks like it's going to be a beautiful evening.

The clear skies also mean I can take a quick swim in the pool. Once I'm at the house, I make sure to set the alarm and then run upstairs to grab a bikini. I would swim naked, but it's the middle of the afternoon, and I don't know . . . Something tells me to wear a suit.

I have to deactivate the alarm to get to the backyard. It's not a big deal. I'll only be in the pool for twenty minutes, tops.

I quickly braid my hair and then jump in, easily moving with long, slow strokes, gliding through the water.

It's colder now that fall has settled into the Pacific Northwest. The pool isn't heated, but it still feels good against my skin.

I enjoyed Montana so much. Every minute of it was relaxing and exactly what I needed to recharge my batteries. But I missed this pool.

When my hand touches the wall, I tuck under in a somersault, then push off and swim to the other side.

The swim is invigorating. When I stand and push the water from my face, I'm panting hard from the exercise.

Whoever said swimming is an excellent workout wasn't lying.

I blink my eyes open and screech, covering my chest in surprise.

"Holy crap, you scared me!"

"Sorry." Rachel is sitting in one of the lounge chairs, one leg crossed over the other, watching me with calm eyes. She's not jumping up to hug me. She's not smiling.

She's not excited to see me.

Something feels *wrong*.

"What are you doing here?" I walk out of the pool and reach for a towel, trying to stay calm. "I don't think I gave you this address."

"You didn't." Her smile is brittle and cold. "I've known where you were for a while. Donald tells me anything I want to know."

"Of course." I wrap the towel around myself and start to walk toward her, then see the gun in her hand and stop short. "What the hell, Rach?"

"I have to tell you, it's been *seriously* annoying that you've had cops all over the place these past weeks. How's a girl supposed to get close to you when you're guarded better than Fort Knox?"

I tilt my head to the side. "You can always get to me, you just have to call."

"You're pretty stupid, aren't you? You can sing, I'll give you that. And you're a pretty little thing. But you're dumb as a box of rocks."

Rachel is my stalker?

"I can't call ahead when I plan to kill you. That would be stupid."

"K-k-kill me?"

"Well, I'm not holding this gun for my own health." She laughs and stomps her feet on the concrete. "Oh, come on. That was funny."

Since when is Rachel fucking crazy?

And why did I leave my phone inside?

Where are you, Levi?

"So, you've been in Seattle for a while then."

"For as long as you have been. Oh, and the dizziness? The headaches? That wasn't from stress, princess."

"You were *poisoning* me?"

"Yeah, and it would have all gone to plan, but you went to

that fucking doctor and fled to Seattle in the blink of an eye. Must be nice to be rich and able to go anywhere, anytime you want."

"So, what did I do to you exactly?"

"You have what's mine."

I narrow my eyes, completely confused as to what she's talking about.

"Your entire fucking career was supposed to be *mine*. Donald was supposed to give *me* the big break. He'd already taken me on, and then he found you slumming it in a hotel, and you probably fucked him so he'd work for you."

"I didn't—"

"Shut up." Her eyes are manic now. I have no idea who this person is. "Suddenly, any shot I had at being a singer was swept away, and I had to fucking *apply* to be your assistant. How is that supposed to make me feel? To be more talented than you, but I have to fetch your fucking *tea?* I have to clean up after you. I wonder what your fans would think if they found out that you have people do *everything* for you?"

"They'd probably think that's pretty normal, actually."

"You think you're so funny. God, I hate you. I *hate* you!"

She's on her feet now, holding the gun up and aimed at my face. She's going to kill me, and I don't know what to do to stop her.

I don't know if I *can* stop her.

"You thought you could protect yourself from me? Well, you can't. Because I'm smarter than you, and I'm *better* than you, you stupid bitch."

"So, do you think you'll just kill me, and then *you'll* be the famous singer?"

"It doesn't matter what I think! It's none of your fucking business. You'll be dead, and you won't care anyway."

"I don't want to be dead."

"Beg me." She cocks her hip to the side. "Beg me to let you live, and I'll think about it."

"You're sick."

Her face crumples in rage.

"That's not begging me. If you don't fucking beg, I'll shoot you right now. DO IT!"

"No." I shake my head slowly, holding her gaze with my own. "I won't beg for what's already mine, Rachel. But I can promise to help you."

"I don't need your help!"

"Starla!"

I turn at the sound of my name, but then there's a loud *crack*, blinding hot pain, and I'm falling.

Suddenly, everything is dark.

nineteen

Levi

If people would stop interrupting me, I could get the hell out of here and home to Starla. I don't like leaving her alone. I know she thinks that a couple of hours isn't a big deal, and she might be right, but I'd feel better if I were there with her.

"Have a minute?" Jim Parker asks, leaning his head around the doorjamb.

"Not really." I sigh and look up at him. "What's up?"

"Update, but not a great one. We're still not able to find a definitive source for the emails, but I think I found something today. There's one specific thread that's come through a couple of times, not enough that we'd catch it if we weren't looking, but it's there."

"Great, keep pulling it."

"I plan to, just didn't want you to think I was slacking on the job."

"You're here more hours than I am, and there's only three of you in your department. I know you're giving me all the hours you can spare. I appreciate it."

"My pleasure. I think we're getting somewhere. I'm going to stay after for a couple hours and keep working on it. I'll try to charm my way to the source."

"Well, that won't get us anywhere, given you're the least charming asshole I know."

I grin when Jim glares at me.

"Kidding. Thanks, man. I'm going to head out. Starla's home alone."

"I thought she had a full-time detail."

"They were needed elsewhere, and we didn't have anyone else to spare."

"Get home then. I'll call if I find anything."

"Appreciate it."

I clip my holster to my belt and toss my jacket on before locking my office behind me and walking out to the car.

I've written my letter of resignation. I had breakfast with my parents this morning, gave them a heads-up. I know they have concerns, and at my age, I don't have to ask their permission, but I do value their input. They've been married for forty-five years, and they're smart people.

Despite their concerns, they also support my decision. The Lubbock case assured me that homicide is *not* for me. And how can I ever stay here in Seattle, working the job, while wondering if Starla is safe, wherever she is?

No, I've made my decision, and now I have to talk with Starla about it, get her input before I quit a job that's been more than good to me for most of my life.

As I turn the corner to Starla's house. Something feels . . . *wrong.*

I don't see anything out of the ordinary. Starla's Jag is in the driveway. No other cars are parked on the street. I glance at Wyatt's house, but it's quiet as well.

I park and get out of the car, looking up and down the still street. There's no noise. Not even any birds, and that's not normal.

When I approach the front door, I pause, taking in the jimmied lock. The door is cracked. I open it and look inside, but there's no one in the living area.

The alarm is *not* set.

I step back outside and call for backup on my phone, speaking quietly.

"This is Detective Crawford. I need backup ASAP." I give the address, put my phone away, and draw my weapon before walking in again, stopping in the living room to listen.

When I look out the back door to the pool, I freeze. Starla is standing, turned away from me, and a woman is holding her at gunpoint.

"Starla!"

The gun fires, the bullet hits Starla in the chest. She falls back, hits her head, and tumbles into the water.

"Freeze!"

"I don't know if she's dead," the woman shouts, aiming the gun at the seemingly lifeless Starla. "I've been trying to end you for years! Why won't you just die?"

"Throw your gun down!"

The woman moves to squeeze the trigger again, but I fire first, hitting her in the head, killing her instantly.

Blood pools around Starla in the pool, and I instantly jump in and turn her over so her face is out of the water.

"Baby." I pull her to the edge, trying to feel for a pulse.

"Come on, baby, stay with me. Don't you dare die on me, Starla. Come on."

"Seattle Police!"

"Back here!" I yell. "The perp is down, and I need an ambulance for the vic!"

"Jesus," Anderson breathes when he sees me in the water with Starla. "The ambulance is here. Who's that?"

"This is Starla. She has a heartbeat, but she's unconscious. I don't know who the perp is."

"On it."

Cops swarm the area, and before I know it, the medics arrive to help me pull Starla out of the water and onto a gurney.

"Heartbeat is strong," one of them says. "Gunshot wound to the upper left chest. Contusion on the back of the head."

"I'm coming with you," I announce as they wheel her toward the ambulance. I glance back at Anderson. "I'll call to give my report."

"This is Rachel Samuels," he calls after me. "Ring a bell?"

I shake my head, then pause. "She's Starla's assistant. Fuck me."

"Looks like we found our stalker."

$\backsim$

"WHO KNEW A gunshot wound would hurt so bad?" Starla asks. It's three hours later, after the worst hours of my life as they took Starla in for tests and then stitched her up. She's on a good amount of morphine right now.

"You shouldn't be in so much pain now, sweetheart." I kiss her cheek. "They've got you drugged up."

"When it happened," she clarifies. "It *really* hurt."

"I'm surprised you remember it."

"Yeah." Tears fill her beautiful blue eyes. "It was Rachel."

"I know." I kiss her again. "I know, baby. I'm so sorry."

"I don't understand. Why? I was always good to her."

"Did she tell you why?"

"Jealous." Her words are a little slurred. "She was jealous. Mad. Crazy. Loved her."

"I know you did."

"Trusted her, you know?" She turns her blurry eyes up to me. "Hard to trust."

"No one's going to hurt you like that ever again. I promise."

"Love you." Her eyes close. She's been fighting sleep, wanting to be alert to what's going on around her. She needs the rest. She needs to heal.

The bullet went clear through and miraculously missed any major organs or arteries. It was the fall, and the hit on the back of the head, that knocked her unconscious. And if I hadn't pulled her out of that pool, she would have drowned.

But she didn't. She's here, and she's whole, and I'm going to spend the rest of my life keeping her safe.

My phone buzzes with an incoming call.

"Crawford."

"It's Parker. We found our stalker."

I frown. "I know. I should have called you, man. She shot Starla today, and I killed her."

"Oh my God. I'm sorry, man. I hadn't heard. Sounds like Belinda Lanigan was off her rocker."

"Wait. Her name was Rachel."

"No, the person sending all of the emails to Starla is Belinda

Lanigan. Her permanent address is in San Francisco, but I found a short-term lease here in Seattle."

"Jesus." I scrub my hand down my face. "Rachel wasn't the stalker."

"Not the email one, no. So, we have a name and an address. Give me the word, and I'll get an arrest warrant."

"Do it."

"On it."

He hangs up, and I can only watch Starla sleep, my brain going a million miles a minute. There were *two* threats. One we had no way of knowing was even in the picture.

I lost about ten years from my life today. The horror of watching the love of my life get shot and not knowing if she was dead or alive was a hell I wouldn't wish on my worst enemy.

It gives me all-new empathy for Jeremy Lubbock and what he walked into.

"Hey."

I look up to see my mom standing in the doorway.

"Mom."

I stand and pull her in for a hug. I know it sounds childish, but having her here is a balm to my hurting heart.

"How is she?"

"She's going to be fine. The bullet went straight through. She has a concussion, and she'll be sore for a while, but she'll be good as new before too long."

"Oh, thank goodness." Mom wipes a tear from her eye and leans in to kiss Starla's forehead. She's sleeping peacefully, but Mom whispers to her. "We all love you, sweet girl."

"Is everyone here?"

"Yes, the whole crowd is out in the waiting room."

"Paparazzi?"

"No. Your officer friends made them leave. And after the tongue-lashing they gave those idiots, I don't think they'll be back anytime soon."

"Good."

"How are you?"

"Relieved. Tired."

"You took a woman's life today, son. And even if she had it coming, that won't sit well with you."

"No, it doesn't. But she was about to take another shot at Starla, and she probably would have killed her. I didn't have a choice."

"No. You didn't. Remember that."

She takes my face in her hands and smiles up at me.

"I'm so proud of you."

"Thanks, Mom."

"If you need anything, just call."

I nod and watch her walk out of the room.

"I like your mom."

I hurry back to Starla and take her hand in mine.

"I didn't know you were awake."

"I was eavesdropping. She kissed me."

"She's an affectionate woman."

Starla's lips tip up in a soft smile. "That's where you get it."

"Yeah." I take her hand in mine and kiss it. "Everyone's here to make sure you're okay. The guys booted the paparazzi out."

"It's good to have people watching your back."

"You have a lot of those people."

"I thought Rachel was one of them." She sighs. "It makes me sad."

"It's okay to be sad. You should be."

"Will you stay with me?"

"I have nowhere else to be. But there will be rules."

She opens one eye, just a slit.

"What rules?"

"You have to sleep. Sleep is going to help you get better."

"And?"

"And no flirting with the male nurses."

"Done."

twenty

Starla

"You're not supposed to be up."

I glower at Jax, who's been bustling around Levi's apartment all morning, cleaning and cooking for me like a mother hen. If I weren't so sick of *staying put*, I'd find it adorable.

"I'm sick and tired of being babysat, Jax. I'm feeling much better. Go home."

"If I leave you alone, you'll overdo it, and Levi will kill me. So, sorry, little girl, you get to be lazy. I'll bake you cookies."

"No more cookies." I shake my head as if he's making me eat salamanders. "Please. Give me a carrot. Or some broccoli."

"You're weird," he says, shaking his head. "I'll give you broccoli if you're a good girl."

"*I'm* weird? Did you just hear yourself?"

He laughs as he walks away. My phone rings.

"Help me. Jax is trying to force-feed me cookies," I say as I answer.

"Poor baby," Levi says with a laugh. "Save some for me."

"You can have *all* the cookies. Are you on your lunch break?"

"I don't take lunch breaks. I'm actually calling because I was wondering how you're feeling today. Do you feel like getting out? I need to show you something, but it's not fun."

"Oh. Yeah, I can come."

"I'll send you an address. Have Jax drive you, okay?"

"Yes, sir. I can't *wait* to be able to drive my own damn car again. It's been two weeks! I haven't taken any prescription meds in like ten days."

"Soon. Now, don't argue with me."

"Bossy cop."

I hang up and call out for Jax. "Field trip!"

"JESUS," JAX BREATHES as we stand in the living room of an apartment not far from the house I rented from Natalie. "She is *weird*."

My photo is everywhere, taped to every square inch of the walls. Some are Photoshopped to show me dead, and others aren't altered at all. It looks like a murder board with photos and maps and strings that connect them all.

"So, the whole time, Belinda was living here, stalking me."

"Since you came up from LA, yes."

"And Rachel did the same thing," I clarify.

"We believe so."

"I'm damn popular," I mutter and rub my forehead with my fingertips. "How did Belinda hide so well?"

"She's been in the computer field forever," Levi says. "She could reroute and hide and do all the things I don't understand.

But she confused our best IT guys for weeks. She was arrested the night of the shooting, and she confessed to everything. She had a breakdown. She's going away for a long time. Whether that's in prison or a mental institution, I don't know."

"It's interesting, the things that make people crazy," Jax says. "Jealousy. Tragedy."

"Illness," Levi adds. "It boils down to illness."

"Yeah," I breathe. "Will I have to testify?"

"No. There won't be a trial. She'll be sentenced in a few weeks."

"So, it's all over? We can finally move on with our lives."

"It's over."

"THERE'S SOMETHING I'VE been meaning to talk to you about," Levi says later that night as we're curled up together in bed, watching a movie on Netflix.

"What?"

"Let me ask you something first." He pauses the TV and sits up on the bed, facing me. "How would you feel about me leaving the force?"

I don't want to get too excited too soon. This might not mean what I hope it does.

"It depends on why you want to quit."

He glances down at my hand before scooping it up in his, giving it a squeeze.

"I want to quit and be the head of your security."

Now, *this* I wasn't expecting.

"Keep talking."

"I have no desire to do the long-distance relationship thing with you, Starla. I'll be here, working the job, and you'll be . . . where? All over the world. And I won't know if you're safe. The guys you've had working for you are incompetent at best. I can protect you better than anyone else. And be *with* you in the process."

I nod, considering it. I would absolutely feel better if Levi were in charge of my safety.

"So, how would we do this?" I ask. "You'd be with me as my employee?"

He licks his lips and leans in to kiss my cheek. "I'd be with you as your confidant." Kisses my nose. "As your lover." Kisses my chin. "As your friend."

He kisses my lips now, long and slow. We haven't been intimate since I was shot, and I miss him so much it hurts.

But when I reach for him, he pulls back far enough to look into my eyes.

"And I'd be with you as your husband, if you'll have me."

The breath leaves my lungs. "What?"

He reaches into the bedside table and comes back with a gorgeous, simple diamond ring.

"Marry me, sweetheart. And not just because I need to protect you, but because I need *you*. Your love, your humor, your light. You make me a better man in a million little ways, Starla, and I can't wait to spend the rest of my life showing you how much I love you. I want a life with you. Whether that life is here in Seattle, in Montana, or on the road three hundred days a year, I don't care, as long as I'm with you."

I cup his cheek and smile into his sweet brown eyes. "You are the greatest man I've ever known in my life, Levi Crawford, and it would be my honor to be your wife."

He slides the ring on my finger and kisses the breath out of me.

"I guess I'll be changing my name again," I say as I stare at the beautiful ring.

"What do you mean?"

"Starla Crawford."

"But you're just *Starla*."

"If people know what's good for them, they'll call me Mrs. Crawford."

He laughs and kisses my hand, just above the ring.

"You're such a diva, darling."

"No, I'm territorial."

All it Takes

New York Times and *USA Today* bestselling author Kristen Proby's second novel in her Romancing Manhattan series delivers the sizzling story of a playboy who's vowed never to commit until he meets the one woman he's tempted to break his promise for.

Quinn Cavanaugh doesn't do anything halfway. He drives fast, works hard, and plays even harder. And the word "commitment" doesn't exist in his dictionary. He has no plans of settling down with one woman for he needs to be free to move on to the next big thing-whatever or whoever that may be. Each party knows the score going into it, and it's all been working out fine. That is, until a sexy new colleague enters the scene.

Sienna Hendricks doesn't give much thought to Quinn and the revolving door leading to his bedroom. She's way too picky about who she shares her time or her body with and screwing around with a colleague isn't part of her plan either. Quinn doesn't intimidate her. And unlike most other members of her sex, she doesn't melt into a puddle at his feet whenever he's near. Most importantly, she has no issues telling him no.

But for a man who has the world at his feet, Quinn isn't accustomed to being rejected. And he's not about to let that change-no matter how persistent Sienna is. To his surprise,

Sienna is everything he thought he'd never find. Pursuing her, and convincing her he's changed, is going to be the biggest challenge of his life. One he's completely up for…

All It Takes releases July 30, 2019

NEW YORK TIMES BESTSELLING AUTHOR
KRISTEN PROBY
USA TODAY BESTSELLING AUTHOR
K.L. GRAYSON

Falling in love is easy...

New Hope, South Carolina is my home. It's where I grew up, got into trouble, and fell in love for the first time. Scarlett Kincaid was more than the girl next door, she was my best friend, until she decided that small town life wasn't for her. One minute she was here, and the next she was gone.

The girl I used to fish with down at the creek is now the biggest name in country music. She headlines world tours, has won four Grammy's, and I haven't seen her since. Until today when she sped through town in her fancy car. One look at her big brown eyes was all it took to stir up a whole slew of emotions. Emotions I'd long ago buried and sure as hell don't have time for.

It's the aftermath that's hard...

There are two things in my life that matter. My music, and my dad. Twelve years ago, I packed a bag and chased my dream.

Leaving New Hope and escaping the gossip mill was the easiest decision I ever made. I never planned to return, but my father needs me, and he always comes first. So, I did what I had to do. I cut my tour short and came home, despite having a sister who hates me, and a community that doesn't trust me. And then there's Tucker Andrews.

When he propped an arm on the roof of my car, pulled down his sunglasses and flashed his police badge, I nearly swallowed my tongue. Gone is the lanky boy who used to throw rocks at me and pull my pigtails. Tucker is now a six-foot package of brawny, sexy man wrapped in more muscle than I have hit singles. Did I mention he's a cop and a single dad?

My goal was to help Dad, and get back to my life. But what am I supposed to when the life that used to strangle me suddenly fits like a glove, and makes me dream of things I never thought I'd have? What happens when the boy I walked away from years ago becomes one of the most important people in my life? I don't have room for a man much less love.

Right?

Because it's impossible to hold onto someone who's already gone.

Already Gone releases August 27, 2019